'No...NO!' I screamed, and pulled away violently. I leapt to my feet. I fought to catch my breath. *Why couldn't I breathe?*

'I'm s-sorry...I can't...' I ran to the door.

He was there before me, facing me, his back against the door. Stunned I stared at him. A moment ago he'd been sitting on the bed.

'How...?' I shut up. Then I tried again. 'Andrew, I can't do this. Please understand. You're going too fast. I'm frightened.'

'Trust me.'

Malorie Blackman is one of the first generation of British-born black writers. Her first book was *Not So Stupid!* (Livewire, 1990) and her books have won several awards, including: the WH Smith's Mind-Boggling Book Award for *Hacker* (1994); the *Young Telegraph* Children's Book of the Year Award for both *Hacker* and *Thief* (1996); and the Stockport Children's Book of the Year Award for *A.N.T.I.D.O.T.E.* (1997) and *Tell Me No Lies* (2000). *Pig-Heart Boy* won the UKRA Award (1997), as well as being shortlisted for the 1998 Carnegie Medal, and was made into a successful BAFTA-winning BBC children's drama. In 1997 Malorie was awarded the Excelle/Voice Readers Children's Writer of the Year Award. Her latest book for teenagers is *Noughts and Crosses* (2001) and she now lives in Kent.

Trust Me

MALORIE BLACKMAN

Livewire
from The Women's Press

First published by Livewire Books, The Women's Press Ltd, 1992
A member of the Namara Group
34 Great Sutton Street, London EC1V 0LQ
www.the-womens-press.com

Reprinted 2001

British Library Cataloguing-in-Publication Data
A catalogue record for this book is available from the British
Library.

ISBN 0 7043 4931 0

Printed and bound in Great Britain by Cox & Wyman Ltd, Reading,
Berkshire

To Neil, with love
And to my favourite sister, Wendy

One

'I'm going on holiday with Andrew and that's final.'

'Heather, I won't allow it.' Her lips thinned with prudish rage. She marched up and down in front of me, wearing a noticeable trough in our grey carpet. I glared at her. I'd spent days rehearsing exactly how and when I'd tell Mum that Andrew and I wanted to go on holiday together. The hours spent in front of my bedroom mirror, practising the right words, the diffident tone, the conciliatory look – all a complete waste of time. I'd started off by saying the wrong thing in the wrong way and we'd gone downhill from there. I took a deep breath and tried again.

'Mum, I'm seventeen, not seven. Anyway, you can't stop me,' I said. Only that came out wrong too.

'While you live under my roof you'll do as I say,' she stormed. And, of course, that did it! I'd lost count of the number of times I'd heard the 'under my roof' threat.

'If I had any sense, I'd be out of here in a second. All you do is nag and criticise and . . .'

'Don't talk to me like that, Heather.'

'But it's all right for you to shout at me and dictate to me, is it? You're always trying to run my life. Run my life? Ruin it, more like.'

'That's not true.'

I didn't let her finish. 'Yes it is. You don't trust me enough . . .'

Now it was her turn to interrupt. 'Listen to me, Heather Lucas. I've lived longer than you, so all I'm

1

trying to do is stop you from making the same mistakes I made.'

'How is going on holiday with Andrew a mistake?' She wasn't even trying to understand.

'You're too young,' she replied instantly. 'You and Andrew are only seventeen and you expect to go on holiday together, *alone*? Well, I won't allow it.'

'How come I'm old enough to work and pay taxes and get married and have children, but I'm not old enough to go on holiday for three lousy weeks?'

'Because I said so. Besides, you couldn't get married without my permission.' Mum raised her hand when I would have butted in. 'And I don't want to hear a damned word about Gretna Green!'

'Mum, Andrew and I have more than enough money between us, we've worked out our exact route and we know where all the British Embassies are should we run into any problems. We're being *responsible*.' I threw her favourite word back at her. Mistake!

'Was it responsible to wait 'til now to tell me? You swan in here, tell me you're going abroad with Andrew this weekend and I'm supposed to *like* it?' Mum sniffed. 'Mind you, I should be grateful you told me at all. Knowing you, I'm surprised you didn't just go away with Andrew and send me a postcard telling me what you'd done and where you were.'

'Well, if you're going to joke about it . . .'

'Do you see me laughing?' she asked coldly.

No, I didn't. There wasn't the trace of a smile on her face. All I wanted to do was be with Andrew. Was that asking so much? It was beginning to look like mission impossible.

'Mum, *please* . . . Look, I'm sorry. I know I should've told you before now, but . . . well, I didn't.' Even I could hear how feeble that sounded!

'And I suppose the idea is that it's now too late for

2

me to stop you?' Mum said. Exasperation hardened her voice and lines of discontent creased her face. 'Heather, why are you in such a hurry to grow up?'

'I *am* grown up, Mum. That's what you won't understand. This isn't fair. When you were my age you were independent. You were pregnant with me . . .'

'I was married to your father first – God rest his soul,' she snapped, scandalised. 'And, yes, I was pregnant with you but I was too young. I didn't know anything. That's all I'm saying.'

'The point is, you were making your own decisions, doing your own thing. You still want me to be your little girl so you can tell me exactly what to do all the time. Well, I'm not Jessica you know. You can't tell me how to run my life . . .'

'Don't bring me into it,' my sister protested.

'Stay out of this, Jessica . . .'

'Butt out, you scabby oik . . .' Mum and I had spoken in unison. Jessica folded her arms across her chest and looked sulky. I scowled at my sister with a look that would turn milk sour. Twelve years old and with a sweet, innocent 'snowflakes wouldn't melt in *my* mouth' expression. With huge brown eyes set in an oval face and short, curly black hair she was already gorgeous, and her looks just kept getting better. Jessica was tall and thin and it was obvious that in a few years she'd be a knock-down, knock-out beauty. She made me sick! I turned back to Mum.

'You're not being fair . . .'

'Fair! You're a fine one to talk,' she replied. 'All year I've been talking about the three of us going on holiday together. You wait 'til everything is arranged – the hotel rooms booked, the train tickets paid for – and then tell me that you are going on holiday with Andrew instead.'

'But the second week of our holiday overlaps with the first week of yours. So what am I supposed to do?

3

You tell me how I can be in two places at once and I'll do it gladly. *You're* being totally unreasonable.'

'Unreasonable!' Lips pinched together, Mum stopped striding for the first time that evening. 'I'm being unreasonable! I like that. You didn't even ask me if you could go on holiday with Andrew, you just told me . . .'

'If I'd asked you, would you have said yes?' I asked, knowing the answer.

'Of course not.'

'Exactly! That's exactly why I didn't ask you. Because I knew you wouldn't approve.'

'Heather, you're seventeen. You don't know every-thing, even if you think you do.'

'I'm not talking about knowing everything. I'm not applying for Mensa membership. All I want to do is go on holiday with Andrew for three tiny weeks. I bet if it was Jessica, you'd let her go. Nothing she does is ever wrong.'

'Now wait just a minute . . .' Jessica leapt out of her chair.

'No. If you wanted to go on holiday with the entire Reggae Philharmonic Orchestra, Mum would let you.' I didn't even try to disguise my dislike as I frowned at my sister. 'We both know that you're her favourite . . .'

'Heather, don't talk such rubbish,' Mum snapped.

'Yeah Heather, you know that's not true.'

'Yes it is, and what's more . . .' I didn't get very far.

'Look, this is getting us nowhere,' Mum said. 'Heather, once and for all, are you going to tell Andrew that you're not going on holiday with him?'

'No. I'll do no such thing.'

'I see.'

Mum and I watched each other. We both knew what this was all about. It had nothing to do with the train tickets or booked hotel rooms or anything else. Going on holiday with Andrew would mean being alone with

4

my boyfriend for the first time. That's what Mum couldn't handle. I could guess the sort of thoughts racing through her head. My face began to burn. And that made me even more angry with her.

'Why don't you just come right out and say what's really on your mind?' I challenged. Mum looked at me. Seconds ticked by.

'Jessica, go to your room,' she said, her eyes never leaving my face.

'Why?'

''Cause I said so.'

'You two are going to talk about sex, aren't you? Why do I have to leave just when it's getting interesting?' Jessica complained. Mum turned and gave her one look.

'All right . . . all right . . . I'm going,' Jessica mumbled. She left the room reluctantly, dragging her feet. If my face was burning before, it was heating the whole house now. I could guess what was coming.

'Are you and Andrew . . .' Mum's voice faltered momentarily. 'Are you and Andrew sleeping together?' No beating about the bush, just straight for the jugular. It took all my courage not to look away and study the wallpaper.

'Suppose I tell you we're not?'

Mum didn't answer. She looked like she didn't know what to believe.

'Anyway, what if we are? It's none of your business what we do. This is my life, not yours.' Embarrassment made me spiteful. She turned away from me, but not before I saw the expression on her face. She was hurt.

'I'm sorry. I . . .' I clamped my lips together. I was fighting hard not to feel guilty, but I was losing. Why was she making this so difficult? Now she had both of us feeling miserable.

'All right then. I'm not having sex with Andrew.

There! Are you happy now?' I flung at her. I couldn't take any more. I darted past her out of the living-room.

'Heather, wait . . .' she called after me, but I didn't stop.

I ran up the stairs, taking them two at a time. Once in my bedroom, I turned and kicked the door shut behind me as hard as I could.

Two

I threw myself down on the bed, my head throbbing. Why was nothing ever easy? As if I wasn't nervous enough about going on holiday with Andrew. In spite of the confidence I'd tried to display, this wouldn't be like a school trip or a holiday with Mum – *I knew that*. Andrew and I would have to fend for ourselves, be responsible for ourselves. That thought excited and scared me, all at once.

And then there was the other reason for going on this holiday . . . My face burned just to think of it. I placed my cool hands against my cheeks, wishing, as always, that I didn't embarrass quite so easily.

'Heather, can I come in?' Jessica knocked at my door.

'Bog off, Jessica,' I snapped.

'Please, Heather.' Jessica came into my room. She chewed on her bottom lip, looking uncertain.

'Jessica, am I suddenly talking Japanese?' I sat up and frowned at her. 'I don't want you in here.'

'I'm not surprised.' Jessica wrinkled up her nose as she looked around. 'If this were my room, I wouldn't want anyone to see it either.'

I gave her the filthiest look I could manage. My room might be disgusting, but I certainly didn't need my sister to tell me. Earlier in the year, Mum had decided it was time to redecorate our bedrooms. Mine was at the front of the house next to hers, Jessica's was at the back, past the bathroom. I'd decided to do my room using anaglypta wallpaper which I'd then paint over. We all went to the DIY megastore together. Mum disagreed with my choice from the moment she saw it.

'You're not really going to paint your room that colour, are you?'

'What's wrong with it?' I was immediately on the defensive.

'Isn't it a bit . . . relentless?'

'What does that mean?' I frowned. 'I think it's quite pretty. It's called Rich Tone Pink.'

'You should get a paler shade. You won't like that once it's glaring at you from all four bedroom walls.' Of course, that did it. I was determined to have Rich Tone Pink or nothing.

And Mum was right. Once I'd painted my bedroom, I hated walking into it. It was like walking into a giant tub of strawberry ice-cream, so I covered as much of the wallpaper as possible with arty Van Gogh, Monet, jazz and whale posters. (I'm into whales.)

'Jessica, what *do* you want?' She frowned down at her feet. The only sound in the room was the ticking of my alarm clock.

'I . . . er . . . will you help me with my school project? I'm having trouble.'

'Get Mum to help you. I'm not in the mood. Close the door on your way out.' That wasn't what she'd wanted to say, I could tell, but at that moment I didn't particularly care. Jessica stood there, looking at me.

'Heather,' she said at last, 'don't you want to come on holiday with us?'

'Of course I do, Jessica,' I sighed. 'I'd love to. But I want to go on holiday with Andrew too.'

'And you want to do that more?'

'I suppose so.' I shrugged.

'Why?'

'Look, I've been on holiday with you and Mum lots of times, but I've never been on holiday with Andrew.

Ireland is beautiful, but we always stay in the same hotel and do the same things, meet the same people – year in, year out, ever since before Dad died. I'd just like to do something different for a change, that's all. And I want to be with Andrew. Do you understand?' Jessica shook her head. Sighing, I lay down on my bed, my hands behind my head and stared up at the ceiling.

'You will when you get older.'

'No, I won't. I wouldn't want to be with some scabby boy instead of you and Mum. You're really horrible, you are.' She sniffed. 'I wish you weren't my sister.'

'I often wish the same thing,' I said, without looking at her.

'You're so rotten these days. I heard Mum tell Mrs Tout that ever since you started going out with Andrew you've been a real pain in every single part of her body,' Jessica shouted. 'And Mum's absolutely right. You're a pain in every single part of my body too.'

'Mum had no business discussing me and Andrew with the neighbours.' I sat up and glared at Jessica. 'And I couldn't care less what you think, you little maggot. Now get out of my room.'

'Won't! And if going out with boys makes you that nasty, then I'll never do it. Never, ever. I'm sorry you ever met Andrew. I hate him.'

Jessica's words shocked me. They shouldn't have, but they did. Recently it'd felt like Andrew and me against the whole world, and it wasn't the romantic feeling some songs try to convince you that it is.

'Jessica, get out.'

'Won't, won't, won't.'

'Fine. Right. Stay here then. *I'll* go out, and as far away from you and this house as I can get.' I stood up and pulled my black leather jacket out of the wardrobe. First, a glance in the dressing-table mirror to smooth down my hair. A glance was all I ever did when it came to looking at myself in the mirror. I had Sasquatch feet, what I liked to call an '*à la Rubens*' figure, and a face that only just made it past reasonable. I had good eyes though, or so I'd been told by my closest girlfriend Diane and a couple of unoriginal boys trying it on. My eyes were almond-shaped and big, the irises so dark brown as to appear black. And I had all my own teeth!

When I was in the fourth year, Gavin Skelly told me that when I smiled it looked like I had a full set of at least three people's teeth crammed into my mouth. For at least a year after that, every time I laughed, I'd lower my head or cover my mouth with my hand. Then one day, I'd had enough of hiding. I said to myself, 'Heather, are you really going to let a dork like Gavin Skelly change your life for you?' The answer was a definite NO! It took over a year to cure myself of hiding my mouth when I laughed, but I *did* it.

One final check to make sure that I had no food caught between my teeth, and I was ready to leave. Then I saw Jessica's face reflected in the mirror. She was watching me, her lips turned down, her expression unhappy. But when I turned around, she just looked sulky. Frowning, I wondered if I'd imagined the look on her face. I didn't think so.

'Look, squirt, I'm sorry I'm not going on holiday with you. I'm going to miss you and Mum, honest I am.'

'I didn't mean it about hating Andrew,' Jessica muttered at last.

'I know. Tell you what, I'll help you with your school project when I get back.'

'Where are you going?'

'None of your business, nosy ratbag.' I pushed past her and down the stairs. Jessica followed behind me.

'Mum . . . MUM! Heather's going out!'

Mum emerged from the living-room as if jet-propelled, her blue pleated skirt swirling around her calves.

She still had the *Guardian* in her hand. She pushed her glasses further up towards the bridge of her nose.

'Where are you going, Heather?'

'Out.'

'Out where?'

'Just out.'

'Heather . . .'

I breathed deeply. Then I spoke slowly and clearly. 'I don't know where I'm going yet. I thought I'd go for a walk. Any objections?'

'Good riddance,' Jessica piped up from behind me.

Mum shook her head at me before going back into the living-room. I stared after her. I felt like I'd been dismissed. Furious, I slammed out of the house. Once my feet hit the garden path, I started to run. I wanted to get as far away as possible. I ran up the road and kept running, not sure where I was going.

All this just because Mum didn't like my boyfriend. But why didn't she like Andrew? I wasn't asking her to adopt him. All she had to do was give him a chance. She didn't *know* him, as I kept telling her, but that didn't matter because she didn't *want* to know him. And with this holiday business she'd probably dislike him even more now.

I ran and ran until a stitch in my side brought me skidding to a halt. I bent over, gasping for breath. I closed my eyes but I couldn't get her hurt expression out of my mind.

Over the last few months, I'd been totally mean to Mum. What was it Jessica had called me? Really horrible? Well, she was right. I knew it. And I knew why.

Because Andrew's parents were exactly the same as Mum. They didn't really know me but that made no difference. They didn't like me.

I remembered the first time I'd gone round to Andrew's house. He obviously hadn't told his family that I

11

was black. They all gaped at me, their mouths open like drowning fish.

Morgan turned to his brother and said, 'Andrew, you must be joking.'

Mrs Harrison was too shocked to say a word. I thought she was about to hit the deck for sure. At least Mr Harrison tried. He smiled weakly, and shook my hand and said, 'Welcome!' I felt about as welcome as a slice of beef on a vegan's dinner plate.

Since then, Mr and Mrs Harrison and I had barely exchanged three sentences at any one time. Andrew's mum was the worst. Around me, she walked like she had a permanent pong under her nose, her head tilted so far back that I was tempted to walk around with a can of aerosol air freshener – and squirt the whole lot up her nostrils!

Andrew just laughed about it. I did too, but inside, deep inside, there was a place where the laughter didn't reach. I told myself that I shouldn't care – after all I was going out with Andrew, not his parents – but it didn't help. And as for Andrew's brother Morgan – just saying his name left a sour taste in my mouth; in fact, the less said about him the better.

So I guessed that's why I was mean to Mum. Because she behaved almost the same way when she met Andrew, and I really thought my mum would know better, *should* know better.

I straightened up and sighed as finally my stitch faded. All that running had made me hot and sticky. August was turning out to be hotter than July. I looked up at the clear sky; at least the sun was beginning to set now. The evening had to get cooler. I stood still, admiring the burning pinks and oranges of the sunset for a few moments. Then I remembered where I was. Feeling like a complete lemon, I looked quickly up and down the high street. Luckily no one was watching. I glanced down at my watch. A quarter past eight. I didn't want to go home yet but where could I go? Being on my own didn't appeal at all. Andrew. I'd go to see Andrew.

But Andrew's mother . . .

She was pretty daunting but at that moment I needed to see Andrew badly. Maybe we could go to see a film, or for something to eat. Somewhere where we could be alone. Andrew always made me laugh and, just lately, it felt as if I'd forgotten how. I was so tired of quarrels with Mum and my sister, quarrels that left a bitter taste in my mouth, even after I'd forgotten what they were about in the first place. Mum, Jessica and I had always been close, but that was all changing and I was at a loss as to how to stop it. Andrew . . . Andrew would cheer me up. As for Mrs Harrison, I'd just have to bite my lip, hold on to my temper and put up with her. My mind made up, I set off.

Three

'Mum hates the idea of us going on holiday together,' I said, sitting on his bed. With my index finger I traced the moss-green spirals and swirls on his duvet cover.

'Does that mean you're not going?' Andrew asked seriously.

'No. It's my life, not my mum's.' I shrugged, then laughed. 'Maybe she thinks you'll abandon me somewhere in the back of beyond for some blonde bimbette with big boobs.'

'Never. You're my one and only bimbette. Besides, your boobs are most acceptable,' Andrew teased.

'That's 'cause I'm wearing my cattle-drive bra.'

'Your what?'

'My cattle-drive bra. It rounds them up, herds them together . . .'

'And moves them out? Heather, that's dreadful!'

'I know. Thanks.'

'You're welcome. I mean it though, you're all I've got – that's worth having at any rate.'

'What about your brother Morgan?' I tried to keep a straight face but failed miserably. We fell about laughing.

I love it when Andrew laughs. He laughs with his whole face, not just his eyes. He's very Celtic looking. Jade green irises with specks of brown and coal black hair. I smiled at him, then lowered my gaze, afraid I was drooling.

'So, have your parents got used to the idea?' I asked, my smile fading.

14

Andrew's pause before answering was just a tad too long. 'Dad thinks we're responsible people so he doesn't mind so much. Mum . . . Well, it doesn't matter what either of them thinks really,' he finished lamely.

'Our mums aren't making this very easy for us,' I sighed.

'That's up to them. We're off on holiday this weekend and there's nothing your mum or my parents can say to stop us.'

'Are you sure about that?'

'Positive.' He looked at me and I looked down at the duvet, still tracing the patterns with my finger. We sat in silence. I had something on my mind that was taking its time getting to my mouth. At last it arrived.

'Andrew, I . . . I'm really nervous about our holiday. I'd be lying if I said I wasn't.'

'Heather . . .'

'No, let me finish.' I had to get this out into the open. 'Andrew, you know how I feel about you and you already know that I've . . . well, I've never . . . been with anyone before but . . .'

'But you're nervous,' Andrew put his hand under my chin and raised my head, 'and getting grief from your mum, and then there are my parents, and you're wondering if maybe we aren't rushing things a bit.'

'What makes you so smart?' I nodded, and sighed with relief.

'Burgers, milk shakes, all kinds of junk food! That and . . . caring about you. Heather, I want to go on holiday with you, be alone with you. I want to . . . well, make it with you.' Two spots of colour appeared on his cheeks. 'But if you decide you're not ready, then I can wait.'

'Yeah?'

'Yeah,' he said firmly. 'Just as long as we still go on holiday. I think we both need a break.'

'So you still want us to go away together?'

'Of course. Don't you?'

I nodded and looked down again.

'Andrew...' I wasn't sure how to continue. 'Andrew, why are you...going out with me?' My face started to burn as soon as the words were out. My fingers were even busier over the duvet cover than before. The room went suddenly very quiet.

'No, never mind. It doesn't matter.'

'Doesn't it?'

I glanced up at him.

'Doesn't it?' he prompted again when I didn't answer. 'Heather, I'm going out with you because I love you. You know that.'

'You didn't love me when you first started going out with me.'

'No, but I liked you a lot. You're intelligent...'

'A Weakest Link contestant.'

'You make me laugh...'

'I can't help the way I look.'

'Beautiful...'

'Especially from behind.'

'You're the only one who listens to me...'

'The list is endless.'

'And you never take anything seriously,' Andrew said, exasperated.

'I can't take that load of twaddle seriously,' I scoffed.

'Then what will you believe?' Andrew asked.

'Your answer to my next question.' I looked down again. I was getting to know that duvet cover really well.

'I'm not...' I couldn't think of how to frame the question. Spit it out, Heather, I thought to myself. 'Andrew, I'm not just an...experiment into exotica, am I?'

16

I glanced up. Andrew's smile had vanished. 'Who told you that? My brother?'

'Morgan has nothing to do with this,' I lied.

'Who then? My mum? Your mum?'

I shook my head. 'Just someone. Does it matter?'

'Yes it does. I'm fed up to the back teeth with everyone sticking their nose into my business and telling me what I should do and how I should do it.'

'You still haven't answered my question.' Andrew's face grew redder and redder as I watched. His whole body was taut. He was about to blow a fuse.

'Calm down. I only wondered. Look, forget I even said anything . . . '

'Of course that's not why I'm going out with you.' His voice was lower and deeper than usual. He really was angry. 'If I were after exotica, I could do a bit better than a girl from Catford vho goes to the same school as me and who is about as exotic as a plate of fish and chips.'

'Thank you very much!'

'I mean it.'

I raised my eyebrows. 'That makes me feel a whole lot better.'

'You know what I mean.' A trace of a smile flitted reluctantly over Andrew's face.

'Yes, I know.' I smiled.

'So exactly which part of you is meant to be exotic?' The trace of a smile faded into annoyance.

'My belly button. Forget it. It doesn't matter.'

'Who said that to you?' he persisted.

'I'm not saying,' I shook my head. 'You'd only go and do something silly.'

'After all these months of going out together, I'm surprised you even had to ask.'

'Andrew, I know you're angry but don't get the hump

with me. I never said it.' It took a few moments for what I said to sink in.

'Sorry!' he mumbled at last.

'Wow! I bet that hurt!' I grinned. Saying sorry wasn't one of Andrew's strong points!

'You'll never know how much.' We both started smiling.

'Andrew, would you and your friend like something to eat?' Andrew's mum thrust open the door and then knocked. (I don't know what she hoped to catch us doing!)

'Heather, are you hungry?' Andrew asked me. I shook my head.

'Well, if you're sure, Andrew,' Mrs Harrison said in her cut-glass voice. She took a quick look around the room before leaving reluctantly. I stared at the door, fighting, and failing, to keep the frown off my face.

'Why does your mother never ask me any questions directly?'

'She does,' Andrew said, surprised.

'Horse manure! Your mother doesn't even look at me.'

'Don't talk wet!' He laughed.

'I'm not. Your mum's not very subtle is she.'

'She's more subtle than your mum.'

'And just what does that mean?'

'Nothing. Never mind. Can we drop the subject?'

'No! We cannot drop the subject.' I glared at Andrew.

'Look, Heather, I don't want to argue with you.'

'You never do,' I snapped. Sometimes I wondered if Andrew's motto wasn't 'anything for a quiet life'.

'What does that mean?' His voice went quiet.

'Never mind . . .'

Silence.

'God! We're not turning into our parents are we?'

Andrew said, appalled. We both creased up laughing at that. The bedroom door flew open again.

'Andrew, are you sure there's nothing I can get you?' his mum asked.

'You asked us that about two seconds ago.' He frowned.

'Did I?' Mrs Harrison smiled brightly. 'I'm sorry, darling, but if I don't pester you to eat you just won't do it.'

'For God's sake, Mum, don't fuss.'

Mrs Harrison fixed her son with an unblinking stare and a painted-on smile. I glared at her, willing her to turn her head and look at me, acknowledge my presence. Just a quick glance would do. She turned with a forced laugh and left the room.

'Why is it whenever I come to your house I feel like I'm either a ghost or I'm having an out-of-body experience? You seem to be the only one in your family who can see me,' I fumed.

Andrew sighed. I opened my mouth to have a good rant but Andrew kissed me, mainly to shut me up I reckon, but a kiss is still a kiss.

I put my arms around his neck and kissed him back. If anyone had told me a couple of years ago that I'd be kissing spotty, snotty Andrew Harrison whom I'd known since Junior school, I would have laughed in their face – either that or chucked up! Andrew Harrison, who turned lobster red in the weakest sunshine and who used to be so wet that you had to swim around him. But here I was, kissing him, and enjoying it. Until the bedroom door flew open for the *third* time.

'Andrew dear, your Aunt Jayne is on the phone. She wants to speak to you.'

That did it!

'I'm going now, Andrew,' I said, standing up. I was probably playing straight into Mrs Harrison's hands –

leaving was just what she wanted me to do – but I was angry. If I gave in to the spite I felt, I would've sat on Andrew's bed and not moved until well after midnight.

'Heather, don't go.' Andrew sprang off the bed and put his hands on my shoulders.

'I've got to,' adding for his ears only, 'I promised Pete I'd meet him at the Burger Bar.' Actually my friend Diane had told me that a whole group of my classmates were going down there for a meal after going to the local cinema. But Andrew didn't have to know that.

'Why're you meeting Pete?' Andrew was furious. I love it when he gets jealous. And he always does!

'Andrew, Aunt Jayne is on the phone,' his mum reminded him. 'She wants to speak to you.'

'Stuff Aunt Jayne!'

'Andrew!' Mrs Harrison was shocked.

I took a quick glance in her direction. Now her eyes were on me, her stare accusatory. *Don't look at me*, I thought sourly. *Your son said it, not me.*

From her look I could tell that she thought it was my fault. Not only did I lower the tone of her household, but of her son's manners as well. I picked up my jacket from where it had been flung over the bedroom chair.

'Andrew I'm not coming back here again, so don't bother to ask me,' I said quietly.

'Heather, wait.' Andrew grabbed my hand before I could leave the room.

'Andrew . . .' said Mrs Harrison. 'Your aunt . . .'

'Hang on a minute, Mum,' Andrew said angrily. 'Just wait here, Heather. Please. Two minutes. Just 'til I get rid of my aunt. *Please.*'

'Oh, all right then.' Why was it that all Andrew had to do was say please and I'd give in and crumble like a stale ginger biscuit.

You're too soft, I thought with a sigh.

He left the room and I heard him run down the stairs.

20

I was about to sit down on his bed until he came back when I realised I wasn't alone. Mrs Harrison was just inside the doorway, watching me. I regarded her, determined not to look away first, even though she had every hair on my body prickling.

'Is something wrong?' I asked.

'Yes, and I think you know what it is. Whilst Andrew's downstairs, I think you and I should have a little chat.'

Four

'A chat about what?' I asked, feigning ignorance.

Mrs Harrison carefully shut the bedroom door behind her. Why was I reminded of a spider's web? She straightened up to look me over, up, down and sideways.

Don't lose your temper, Heather, I had to tell myself over and over again.

'I don't want you to go on holiday with my son,' Mrs Harrison said with no messing about. Just shoot to kill.

'Why?' I tried to keep my tone pleasant.

'I don't want Andrew to get hurt.'

I counted to ten. Then counted to ten again. I smiled. 'I don't understand. How is Andrew going to get hurt by going on holiday with me?'

'You're not right for him. And suppose you get into trouble? I don't want Andrew's life ruined.'

Get into trouble? Quaint!

'What trouble could I possibly get into if Andrew's with me?'

Mrs Harrisons lips were so thin as to be practically non-existent. I glared at her.

'Ah, I get it. You don't want any non-white babies polluting the Harrison blood line – isn't that what you mean?'

Mrs Harrison went pale and stared at me. I'd shocked her and I wasn't sorry either, but to tell the truth I was a little surprised at myself. I hadn't realised I'd said it out loud until I saw the look on her face.

'That's not what I said,' she replied.

But that's what you meant, old cow!

22

'Then how am I – what was it you said? – "not right for him"?'

'Because . . . because you're . . . just not.'

Coward! Why not be honest? Why don't you just come right out and say it . . . I'm black and he's white and never the twain . . . I thought to myself.

'Heather, I'm asking you to tell Andrew that you've changed your mind about going on holiday with him.'

'But I haven't. So why should I lie.' I would have had more respect for her if she'd just come right out with what was on her mind.

'Do you know what you're doing to my family? All any of us do these days is argue about you.'

That spiteful remark found its target. And it hurt. First home, now here. I stared at the resentful look on her face. I'd seen the same look earlier that day, on my mum's face.

'Heather, I . . .' The door was pushed open and Andrew strode into the room, only to freeze when he saw his mum and me regarding each other. I looked down at the carpet, thrusting my hands deep into my jacket pockets.

'I'm leaving now. I'll see you tomorrow.' I spoke quietly.

'Mum? What've you been saying?' Andrew asked.

'Forget it, Andrew,' I said, moving forward.

He was glaring at his mum now. Me? I was tired.

'I've had about enough of this. Mum, back off. If I want to go out with Heather, I will and there's not a damned thing you or Morgan or anyone else can do about it.'

'Don't talk to me like that.' Mrs Harrison frowned.

'Heather, come on. We're getting out of here.' He grabbed my arm and pulled me after him past his mother.

Did all parents swallow some kind of pill to turn them into bum holes, I wondered.

And at that moment I missed Dad, very much. He would have been on my side. He always stuck up for me. Okay, so Mum's major objection was that she didn't want me to get hurt, but Dad would've been more optimistic. He always said that if you went looking for grief or failure you were bound to find it. Mum seemed to think that my relationship with Andrew was doomed. It was funny how similar she and Mrs Harrison were in that respect.

Andrew was still pulling me along when we were out of his house and half way down the road. The air was cooler now. A gentle breeze blew over my face. I breathed deeply and let it out as a sigh. The sky was a deep shade of blue and the full moon had turned the few clouds silvery. Here and there, stars twinkled faintly. It was lovely. I remembered Mum telling me, when I was five or six years old, that stars were holes in the floor of heaven. I loved that idea. It was almost as good as the real explanation. I stared up at the sky as we carried on walking. When I tripped over a broken paving stone, I came down to earth.

'Andrew, you're pulling my arm off,' I complained.

'They're driving me nuts!' he hissed. 'I'm beginning to wonder if Mum and Dad didn't have Morgan, and then just find me next to their garden gnome, a couple of years later!'

I'd been wondering similar things myself over the last few weeks but I didn't say anything. Whenever Andrew was in this kind of mood it was best to let him get it all off his chest.

'I've got Dad in one ear, telling me to give Mum a bit longer to get used to the idea of you and me. But then he gives me a load of useless advice about handling women, especially . . . well, never mind. Meanwhile,

Mum's busy whining in the other ear. And then there's Morgan, spouting off in both my ears. If it weren't for my gran and Aunt Jayne, I'd go mental. God, I wish they'd all just leave us alone. These days I feel more like I'm drowning than swimming, except when I'm with you. Sometimes I feel this close,' he held his thumb and index finger together, 'from lashing out, breaking out . . . *something* . . .'

'Andrew . . .' I said softly.

He stopped marching and frowned at me. I kissed him, there and then. Usually, I don't go in for that sort of thing in the street, but at that moment we both needed to be kissed. He sighed and the tirade was over.

'All the same,' I said as we carried on walking together, holding hands, 'I don't think I'll go back to your house again.'

'Because of my mother? Don't let her get to you. She's not worth it. Besides, in three days time we'll be on holiday. Together. Alone. Away from our families. Hallelujah!'

'Your mum doesn't even try to hide the fact that she dislikes me,' I complained.

'Forget her.' He shrugged. 'You're not going to let her chase you away, are you?'

'She's very rude.'

'So's your mum.'

I couldn't argue with that.

'So where are we going?' I asked.

'The cinema? There's that thriller at the local that I'd like to see.'

I wrinkled up my nose. 'Do we have to? I'm not in the mood for a blood-and-guts, slash-'em-up film.'

'You can always hide your face in my armpit like you usually do,' Andrew laughed.

'I wouldn't have to if you didn't insist on dragging

me to those kind of films. You know I don't like them. Can't we go to the Burger Bar instead?'

'Is Pete really going to be there?'

'Probably.' I shrugged.

'Then I'm sticking to you like glue.'

I laughed.

'What have you got against Pete?' I do so love it when Andrew gets jealous. 'I thought you two were friends?'

'We are. But I've seen the way he looks at you.'

'Oh yeah? And what way is that?'

'Like he wants to try taking you out again.'

'Well he can't 'cause I'm going with you now, aren't I?'

'That won't stop him!'

'Of course it will. Pete's a gentleman.'

'And if he isn't?'

'Then *I'll* stop him.'

'I'd still like to punch his face in, just to warn him off.'

'Why don't you then?' I asked coldly. My smile disappeared.

'Because you wouldn't like it,' he replied with a wry smile.

'Too right. That sort of macho crap does *not* impress me.'

'Besides, he's bigger than me,' Andrew grinned.

My hero!

When we walked into the Burger Bar, all kinds of kissing and slobbering and lip-smacking noises assailed us.

'Wonders will never cease! What happened?' Diane asked.

'What d'you mean?' I asked.

'You two have stopped gazing into each other's eyes

26

for long enough to give your poor, neglected friends a moment of your time,' she replied with a smile.

I smiled back, but I knew she meant it. Diane and I had been like Siamese twins, joined at the hip, before I started going out with Andrew. Now I couldn't remember the last time she and I had done anything together. When had we sat down last and chatted, really chatted? Embarrassed, I turned away from her, latching on to the first face in the crowd I saw.

'Hi, Pete. How are you?'

Pete was gorgeous, the colour of strong coffee (no milk!) – just the way I like it! – with the whitest, most even teeth I'd ever seen away from the cinema screen. (I'm into good teeth!) He was six feet two and broad but not fat. All the girls in my year leched after him.

'I'm okay. All the better for seeing you.' He smiled, making everyone, except Andrew, laugh. Pete always talked to me like that. It was strange to think that Pete and I might have been an item now, if he hadn't stood me up on our first date!

'Budge up then,' I said, tapping him on the shoulder.

He shifted, squashing everyone else up. I sat down next to him and Andrew sat down directly opposite me. Andrew looked at me and I looked at him. I couldn't resist a smile and a sly wink. I was sitting next to Pete! Andrew gave a rueful look. He glanced at Pete before turning back to me. He looked . . . nervous. What did he think I was going to do? Explore Pete's leg under the table? I smiled to myself, imagining Pete's reaction. He'd probably jump out of his skin. I gave serious thought to testing out my theory but decided against it. Andrew would only get the hump and I'd had enough grief for one evening.

'Looking forward to your holiday?' Pete asked.

I nodded, then shrugged. Did I look as self-conscious as I felt?

'Is it all sorted out then?' he continued.

'Not quite. Mum's giving me a hard time, but I'm working on her. Did Andrew tell you about our plans then?'

'That's right.' Pete glanced at Andrew.

I looked at Andrew. He was looking at Pete. Our holiday wasn't a big secret but I sort of wished Andrew hadn't told anyone.

'You mean you're actually going? Your mum is going to let you?' Diane was amazed.

Seeing my raised eyebrows, she explained, 'Pete told me.'

I sat back in my chair. 'Is there anyone in this place who doesn't know my business?' The question wasn't altogether a joke.

Everyone laughed and started discussing our holiday. My friends talked about it as if Andrew and I were taking a trip to Sainsburys rather than across Europe. That helped a lot. After ten minutes or so, it didn't seem quite such a big deal.

As I watched Andrew explaining our proposed route, I faded out to think of other things. Such as what it would be like to make love with him.

Oh, we'd kissed and petted but never to the point where I'd got carried away. Fumbling around with the lights off or in dark, secluded places wouldn't be the same as being alone and unrushed and with no threat of interruption. My stomach began to rock nervously at the thought. But I loved Andrew very much and I wanted him, all of him. And I'd sorted out all the embarrassing but necessary bits.

A month ago, I'd finally plucked up the courage to go to the local Family Planning Clinic. It was nowhere near as bad as I'd thought it would be. They took my blood pressure and weighed me, then I had a long chat with one of the doctors. She was really kind and sympathetic. She listened to what I had to say about me and Andrew. I left the clinic with a six-month supply of contraceptive pills and a whole brown bagful of condoms. Andrew and I had only just started discussing going away on holiday together at that stage, but I'd decided it was time to be practical. I had my life all mapped out for the next ten years. I wanted to finish my exams, go to college, get my English degree, take a year out to go around the world, then train to be a teacher or maybe an advertising copywriter. I'd get my own two-bedroom flat, one bedroom for me, the other for all the books I intended to collect, and only when I was pushing forty would I think about settling down. Pregnancy and babies didn't feature for years yet.

'Hey! Heather, penny for them.' Andrew's teasing voice finally reached me.

'They're worth more than that,' I said.

He smiled, then kissed the palm of his hand and blew on it. I caught the kiss and pressed it to my lips.

'Someone pass the bucket, *please*!' Diane grimaced. And everyone else joined in, making puking noises. I grinned at Andrew.

'Ignore them. They're just jealous!' he said.

We were having a great time, a really good laugh. Even Diane started talking to me again. For the first time that night I began to unwind. It was wonderful. Relaxing and easy. Then I happened to glance towards the door and my heart dropped into my shoes. Every muscle in my body pulled taut. My skin began to prickle.

'Oh hell!' I muttered.

Pete heard me. 'What's the matter?'

'There's going to be trouble. Andrew's brother Morgan and his mob have just walked through the door.'

29

Five

'Andrew's brother? So?' Pete asked.

'You don't know Morgan,' I replied grimly. 'He's a real pig. And remember, you heard it here first.'

Morgan looked around. I waited for him to see us. There was going to be bother now. I knew it. If I'd been alone I think that maybe, just maybe, I would have slid down in my seat or, at the very least, hidden my face behind a cupped hand.

'Heather, are you all right?' Pete frowned.

I'd forgotten about him. I glanced at Andrew who was sharing a joke with Diane across the table. I risked a surreptitious glance towards the door. Morgan was heading straight for us, his three stooges close behind him.

'Hiya, little brother. I see you're slumming again,' he said, looking directly at me. Odious git-faced toad! All conversation at our table faded and died.

'It's always great to see you as well, Morgan,' I said, inflecting my voice with as much ice as possible.

'Heather, you look ... the same as ever.'

Behind him, Morgan's cronies grinned like ninnies. Morgan was dressed in his usual uniform: black jeans that only just made it past his hips, an open black shirt over a grubby white T-shirt and sunglasses, even though it was now dark outside. He fancied himself something rotten, strutting around as if his clothes were really the business. I thought he looked ridiculous.

'Morgan, leave Heather alone,' Andrew's voice held patient amusement, as always.

I glared at him. It was always the same. He joked with Morgan, smiled with Morgan – and never took him seriously. He just laughed away all of his insults, like shooing off irritating but harmless flies.

'Andrew, I can't understand why you don't give this . . . this no-class, no-hoper the elbow,' Morgan went on, 'You can do better, brother.'

'Why don't you bog off, Morgan?' I said. I placed my hands on my thighs under the table and stretched out my fingers.

'Andrew, have you thought of giving Battersea dogs home a call? I'm sure they've got a better class of bitch than the one sitting at this table.' Morgan smiled at me.

'But wait . . .' Pete mumbled from beside me.

Don't let him get to you, I told myself. Over and over. Don't let him get to you. But he did.

'Why don't you go and play in the traffic? *Please*. And don't call me a bitch. I'm a woman, not a female dog.'

'You! A woman!' Morgan's laugh was grating and harsh.

'Yes, me,' I replied furiously. 'And if you weren't such a fart-faced, pea-brained git you wouldn't need to be told.'

'Who are you calling a git?' Morgan hissed.

'I got the rest right then, did I?'

'That remark is just about what I'd expect from a slag like you.'

'Slag is rather a big word for you, isn't it – you cretinous pig!' Really childish I know. But Morgan always brought out the best in me. I could feel myself winding up to be *really* insulting. My friends started to giggle.

'Morgan, leave it at that,' Andrew smiled. 'You're

31

only going to lose. Once Heather gets going, she's deadly.'

Morgan looked around the table, then back at me. His bottle-green eyes glinted like cold marble.

'Look at you. No wonder your dad did a runner. I bet he couldn't wait to see the back of you and your family, and who can blame him,' Morgan said scornfully.

I felt like I'd been punched in the stomach. I heard some anonymous gasps before everyone around me went deathly quiet. Pete stood up, his expression furious. I shook my head at him and pulled him down to sit beside me again. I turned to face Andrew. I couldn't breathe, I could hardly think straight. I'd told Andrew about my dad in the strictest confidence and here was his brother, twisting my words and playing them back to me. I hadn't even told Diane about Dad. Just Andrew.

Andrew looked at me, his face red. Deliberately, I turned away from him to face Morgan.

'You keep your filthy mouth off my dad. He's . . . he's dead, so just keep your foul remarks to yourself,' I said quietly. It was as if some almost unbearable weight had been placed on my chest, making each breath an effort. My fingers were stretched out so hard, the joints ached. At least a bucketful of sand had appeared in my throat, choking me, and my eyes were stinging.

'Living on the other side of England wasn't quite far enough from you lot then?' Morgan said, enjoying himself. 'Just *dying* to get right away, was he?'

I sprang up. Morgan grinned at me, a satisfied gleam in his eyes. Before I could think about what I was doing, I slapped his face. The gleam vanished. He stared at me. I was dimly aware of my palm stinging and of Andrew moving to stand in front of me.

'Why you . . .' Morgan moved towards me.

'Morgan, you deserved that. You were right out of order with that remark,' Andrew said sharply. 'I think you'd better go now.'

I wished Andrew would move out of the way. My knee cap was itching to meet Morgan's goolies.

'You'd better keep that slag out of my way.' Morgan jabbed his finger in my direction. I didn't say anything.

'You can thank your lucky stars that Andrew was here to look after you,' said Morgan.

'I can look after myself.'

He glowered at me. I scowled back.

'Watch yourself,' he said quietly.

And off he strode, followed by his sheep, who each directed a filthy look at me before they left the Burger Bar.

'Did you have to do that?' Andrew rounded on me in front of everyone as soon as the door shut behind the last of his brother's idiots.

'What do you mean?' I frowned.

'Don't you think you rather over-reacted? If only you two . . .'

'Over-reacted! Are you serious?' I couldn't believe what I was hearing.

'Why let him get to you? You know what he's like. If you ignored him or laughed at him the way I do, he'd leave you alone.'

I stretched out my fingers again.

'Was I supposed to sit and smile whilst your brother told lies about my family?' I asked slowly. 'And thank you so much for telling him about my dad. Training to be a tabloid journalist, are you? It's nice to know that you can be trusted.'

'Heather, that's not fair.' Andrew moved towards me, his arms outstretched.

I slapped his hands away. Then, without another word, I turned and ran out of the Burger Bar.

33

Six

'Heather, hang on! Heather, I'm sorry!'

Andrew chased after me but I didn't stop running. Inside . . . inside I was bleeding.

'Heather, I'm really sorry.'

He grabbed my arm and spun me around to face him. 'Heather, please. I just happened to mention it at home once. I didn't know Morgan was going to twist what I said like that.'

'Did you tell your family my dad did a bunk to get away from us?' I asked, brushing an imaginary hair out of my eyes. Andrew tried to take my hand in his. I pulled away angrily.

'You know I wouldn't say a thing like that.'

'Then what did you tell them? Go on. I'm all ears.'

Andrew took a deep breath. 'I said that your dad had left for a while but that he came back before he died.'

'I see. And did you tell them how my dad died?'

Andrew opened his mouth but nothing came out. He nodded slowly. 'Heather, I promise you . . .'

I wasn't having any.

'I told you about my dad on the strict understanding that you wouldn't tell anyone else, especially not your family. I *trusted* you. You stabbed me in the back, Andrew. I'd never do that to you. I swear, I'll never tell you anything else again.'

'Heather, I'm sorry. It won't happen again. I . . .'

'I'm going home now.'

'Heather . . .'

'I'm tired, Andrew.'

'Heather, please. I . . . I said I was sorry.'

'You say you're sorry and that makes everything okay now, does it?' I regarded him stonily. 'Sometimes, Andrew, I wonder why I bother with you. I'd do better with Pete . . .'

'Don't say that!' He was furious. 'Don't *ever* say that.'

'Why not? It's true. You can't keep secrets and you don't consider my feelings at all. Sometimes I'm with you, and all I can see and hear is your mother and your brother. You weren't found on their doorstep. You're a Harrison all right.'

I didn't mean it, not really. Not all of it. I just wanted to lash out. But my words had the appropriate effect. Andrew drew himself up and became very still.

'I guess I had that coming,' he said quietly.

I didn't reply. I looked at him, he looked at me. Seconds turned into minutes.

'So . . . are we still going on holiday this weekend or are you calling it off?'

I looked up at the silver moon. The peaceful, uncomplicated life I wanted seemed to be up there with it. Why was nothing ever easy?

'Do you want me to call it off?' I prevaricated.

'No, I don't. I want to be with you, alone with you. We both need to get away.'

That was true. If I had any more days like this one, I'd go loopy. I'd never had a day like it. From the moment I'd woken up, all I'd had to do to start a quarrel was look at someone – and sometimes, not even that much.

'You shouldn't have told your family about my dad,' I sniffed. 'I told you it was a secret.'

'I know. I'm sorry.'

'So what're we doing tomorrow and Friday?' I looked around, anywhere but at Andrew.

35

Andrew thought for a moment. 'How about if I come round to your house tomorrow and talk to your mum?' he suggested.

He had my full attention now. 'Talk to her about what?'

'About our holiday.'

'You must be joking!' I stared at him.

'No, I think I should. I want her to know I'm serious about you. I'd never do anything to hurt you. I want her to know that.'

'I don't know . . .' I said doubtfully.

'Leave everything to me,' smiled Andrew. 'And, Heather . . .'

'Yeah?'

'I'm sorry.'

'So am I, Andrew. So am I.'

The next day, Andrew came to see Mum just as he'd promised, or should I say threatened? We all sat down on the sofa and he brought out our itinerary and various maps. He went through every kilometre of our holiday until Mum knew more about it than I did.

While she still wasn't mad keen on the idea, I think she realised gradually that come hell or high water we *were* going away on holiday together. Andrew stayed at our house all day, in spite of the subtle and not-so-subtle hints I directed at him (like blinking and winking and kicking him in the shins under the dinner table). He ended up having lunch and dinner at our house, something he'd never done before. During dinner, I caught Mum reluctantly smiling to herself. She's no fool and she knew what he was doing. But even so, Andrew's gesture went down better than I thought it would.

Later that evening, after Andrew had gone home, Mum came into my bedroom, shutting the door quietly behind her. I recognised the look on her face from the day before. She was going to talk about sex again. Why did adults of her generation and beyond have such a problem discussing something so normal and natural? Sex. Sex. Sex. The word didn't scare me!

'Heather, I want to ask you something. And it's not because I'm being nosy.'

'I'm listening.'

'Are you on the pill or something?'

There was a moment's silence before I answered. My damned face was beginning to burn again.

'I'm on the pill.'

Mum came and sat down on my bed. 'Since when?'

'Since a month ago.'

'But you're still a virgin?'

'Yes, Mum.'

Hell! Stop sounding so defensive, I told myself.

'Heather, be careful.' Mum sighed. 'I care about you. I don't want to see you disappointed or hurt.'

'I won't be, Mum. I promise.'

She looked like she wanted to say something else but didn't know how to. So in the end she decided to say nothing. She held out her arms and after a moment's hesitation, I moved into them. We hugged, something we hadn't done in a long, long time. It felt strange, like a hug hello or a hug goodbye.

'You won't change your mind?'

'No, Mum,' I sighed.

'You always were stubborn.' She sat back and looked at me. 'Once you've made up your mind to do something, I might as well go and waste my breath arguing with the dustbins outside. I'd get further.'

'You always said my ears are stuck in my backside.' I smiled faintly.

'That's what my mother used to say about me. And it sure applies to you.'

'Now I know where I got my stubborn streak from.' I smiled. 'It's inherited!'

She stood up and walked to the door. Her hand on the handle, she turned around and whispered, 'Enjoy your holiday.'

I couldn't believe it. I'd won. I could go! Instantly, my eyes started stinging. I had to fight to control myself. I couldn't let Mum see me cry. What would she make of that?

'Mum, what would you have done if I hadn't already been to the Family Planning Clinic?'

'I would have gone there with you tomorrow.'

'Oh, I see.'

'Did Andrew go with you?' she asked after a pause.

'No, I went by myself.'

'Next time, get him to go too. It's his responsibility as well as yours.'

I nodded. She left the room. I wanted to call her back, to hug her and hold her and be her little girl again. But I kept silent. I wanted it both ways. Not possible. I was only just beginning to realise it, but I'd made my choice when I said yes to Andrew about going on holiday with him. There was no going back now, even if I wanted to – which I didn't.

Onwards and upwards.

Seven

Andrew came to pick me up at about eight o'clock on Saturday morning. From the time the doorbell rang, my heart tried to beat its way right out of my chest. Jessica said very little to Andrew, Mum said even less, but it didn't matter. I hugged and kissed them both and whispered in Mum's ear, 'Don't worry, I'll be fine. I'll phone.'

'Just make sure you do.'

Andrew helped me put on my back pack. I did up the buckles and turned back to Mum and my sister.

'Bye,' I said. It seemed so inadequate.

'Bye, Mrs Lucas. Bye, Jessica. We'll send you postcards from every place we visit.'

Mum nodded and turned away. Andrew and I left the house. We were finally on our way.

All the way down to the coast, I still couldn't believe that we'd managed it. Even on the deck of the ferry, watching the British coastline disappear, I couldn't quite take it in. This couldn't be real and happening to *me*! I raised my head, feeling sophisticated, mature. I was actually going on holiday with my boyfriend! And then I felt really childish for feeling sophisticated in the first place! I closed my eyes, smelling the salt air and feeling the brisk, cool breeze on my face. It was a beautiful day and it could only get better.

'We're here, Heather,' whispered Andrew. I nodded happily. He put his arm around my shoulders. Then the cramps started.

I unbuckled my back pack and let it fall off my back, all in about three seconds flat.

'I'll be right back,' I gasped, and bolted for the nearest ladies loo.

My worse suspicions were confirmed. I'd thought that being on the pill would ensure that my periods were more regular. Got that wrong in a big way! I closed my eyes and leaned against the door. I wanted to kick it in.

'Heather? Are you okay?'

'Andrew?' I unbolted my cubicle door. 'For goodness sake, this is the ladies loo. Suppose someone comes in.' I looked around anxiously.

'Stuff 'em. What's the matter?'

I looked down at my shoes, my heart pounding, my stomach aching. 'I . . . My period has started. I'm at least a week early,' I said, adding miserably, 'Sorry.'

'What are you apologising for? How're you feeling?'

'Cramp and slight backache, not as bad as usual though. This whole holiday business must have wound me up more than I thought. It's happened before. My cycle also went haywire just before my mock exams.'

'Don't worry about it.' Andrew smiled. 'Do you want me to bring your back pack? I've left it just outside.'

'No, it's okay. I always keep a couple of tampons in my shoulder bag.'

'I'll wait for you outside.'

I nodded. Andrew walked towards the door.

'Sorry, Andrew,' I said after him.

He walked back to me. 'Shut up, Heather. It's not important, I promise. I'm with you and that's what counts.'

'So you're not disappointed?' I frowned. *I'd* be upset if he wasn't just a tiny bit disappointed.

'Maybe just a little,' he said ruefully. 'But, like I told

you before, I can wait.' And he kissed me, slow and deep.

It would have been a long one as well, if some old biddy hadn't chosen just that moment to walk into the loos. Andrew and I sprang apart guiltily. The woman, who must have been at least fifty, with dyed red hair and dark brown drawn-in eyebrows, looked up at the sign on the outside of the door and then back at us.

'Do you mind! These are the ladies toilets!' she frowned.

'I was just going,' Andrew replied. And he scarpered past her.

The woman looked at me. 'I was young once too,' she said, 'but really!'

'Sorry,' I mumbled and darted back into my cubicle.

When I rejoined Andrew on the deck, he grinned sheepishly at me. We didn't say a word, just fell about laughing. He put his arms around me and we kissed again, this time out in the open, so no unexpected interruptions. I was so happy. This was going to be the best holiday of my life. I could feel it.

It began better than either of us had dared imagine. We were armed with our young person's railcards, our book on youth hostels across Europe, and our back packs and enough enthusiasm to sink a continent. We avoided all the major towns and spent our nights in youth hostels, sharing each room we had with at least four other people. Once, when we'd decided to walk to the next town and underestimated our progress, we had to spend the night in our small tent in a field, at least ten miles from the nearest hostel. But even that was fun because it was new and exciting and different – and we were alone! We joined our sleeping bags together and cuddled up. We had a good kiss and cuddle, even though we both had pyjamas on in case someone came along. It was wonderful.

Slowly but surely London and our families and our friends all faded away. And as the rest of the world retreated, so Andrew, and how I felt about him, seemed to take over. All the grief, the arguments, the rough times, they were all worth it. Or rather, Andrew was worth it. A day didn't pass without Andrew telling me that he loved me. Neither of us had really said the words that much before. But now, away from everyone else, it was as if we were two new people.

The first week of our holiday flew by. We were pretty much wrapped up in ourselves, although we did make friends at a couple of the youth hostels we stayed at and exchanged addresses and telephone numbers. But all too soon, we were into the second week of our holiday, with the final week approaching. I didn't want it ever to end.

We changed our plans slightly and swapped our itinerary around. The things we'd planned to do in the third week, we decided to do in the second. Tuesday evening of the second week, Andrew and I arrived in a small town called Fipoli. All the way there on the train, Andrew had this secretive smile on his face. And he wouldn't tell me why. When we got to the youth hostel I found out the reason.

'Hi! I'm Andrew Harrison. This is Heather Lucas.' Andrew smiled at the receptionist.

'*Ciao!* I am Marcus.' The receptionist smiled back. 'You want two beds for the night, yes? You have booked them already?'

'Actually, I booked a twin room,' Andrew said evenly. I stared at him. He didn't bat an eyelid. It was if he did this sort of thing all the time! My face started to burn. I risked a glance at the receptionist, Marcus. He was tall and relatively good-looking, with dark brown hair and quite thick eyebrows. His eyes were friendly, but sharp and he spoke with a very funny-peculiar accent. He was at least thirty-five.

Looking at him I wondered if he could tell I'd never done this before? It felt as if a neon sign of pointing arrows and innuendo had suddenly appeared above my head.

'We arranged the room for two nights next week but we've changed our plans,' Andrew continued. 'I did phone ahead to ask if we could have the room for tonight and tomorrow of this week instead.'

Marcus glanced down at the huge ledger-type book on the desk before him. 'Ah yes, I have it now. We have your twin room available for tonight and tomorrow as requested. There will be a small administration charge for the change of plan as discussed over the phone. Is that okay?'

'Heather?' Andrew looked at me.

I shrugged, looking what I hoped was nonchalant. I too wanted to look as though I did this sort of thing all the time. 'That's okay. We'll take the room.'

'*Bene*! You have your own sheets or you wish to hire some?'

'We'll hire them.'

I listened as Andrew sorted out the rest of the details. We'd actually got a room to ourselves. Wow! For the first time since we'd come on holiday, we'd have a room in a hostel to ourselves.

On our way up, I said, 'I'm very impressed. How did you manage it?'

'Skill, charm, charisma . . .'

'Modesty.' I laughed.

'I found out which hostels in which countries catered for couples and as this one was on our proposed route, I booked the room in advance from London,' Andrew explained.

'You booked it that far in advance? You were very sure of me,' I said slowly.

'No, I wasn't. The beds don't have to be together for us to be together.'

'I guess not.' I shrugged.

It was a tiny room, only slightly bigger than our bathroom back home. The paint was a dingy yellow and peeling off the walls and there were two single beds and an empty wardrobe, that was it. But it was *ours*.

'Here, let me help you get that back pack off,' Andrew said.

I turned my back to him and started to unbuckle the pack. Suddenly, inexplicably, I was nervous. Pigeons in DMs were marching up and down my stomach. Andrew lifted the pack off my shoulders and put it on the floor between the far bed and the window. Then he took his own pack off and placed it on top of mine. We watched each other.

'It's hot in here, isn't it?'

I nodded.

'Fancy a walk and maybe something to eat?'

I nodded again.

'Come on, then.'

'Will our back packs be safe in here?'

'Probably not, but there's nothing in them worth fleecing.'

We left the youth hostel and made our way into the town centre, about a ten-minute walk. I kept thinking, this is it! Tonight is the night. Surprise, surprise! – my face started burning!

The sun had set and the sky was darkening. There was a gentle breeze blowing. We strolled along, hand in hand, window shopping. I looked in the window of a crafts shop. The dull street light behind me cast dark shadows so I had strain to see into the unlit shop window. Then I noticed my reflection. Eyes, obsidian dark and bright, shined back at me. Andrew always said I was useless at hiding my feelings. Every thought, every fear, every emotion shone from my face like an image from a ten-metre high cinema screen. Right now, it was true.

I turned to Andrew and thought, I'm happy. No mistake about it. Really soppy I know, but that's how I felt.

'It's a shame our holiday didn't start sooner. I might have avoided all the unpleasantness with my mum and your mum and your brother and my sister and . . .'

'And the cat and the garden gnome!' he teased.

'And you.'

His smile faded. 'And me,' he agreed quietly. Then he smiled again. 'Still, we're here now and that's all that matters.'

'What presents am I going to get Mum and Jessica and my friends? I'd better think about it now, before my money runs out,' I said.

'Hhmm! When we get back to the youth hostel, I suppose I'd better send a postcard to my mum and dad,' he sniffed. He wasn't very enthusiastic about it. I'd already sent two postcards back home and spoken to Mum once on the phone, but I decided a third postcard wouldn't hurt.

The evening air was warm and the town was still. Very few people were about. The occasional car drove down the main street, but that was it. It made a change from London.

I was just about to turn back to the craft shop window when my stomach started to rumble. Glancing at my watch, I said, 'Andrew, I'm hungry.' I stepped into the road. 'Let's try and find . . .'

'Heather, look out!'

The moment Andrew shouted at me, I heard the blare of a car horn. I turned my head, and saw the car. Like a rabbit in the glare of oncoming headlights, I couldn't move, I couldn't blink, I couldn't even breathe. The car was coming straight for me. Then, all at once, I couldn't see it. The car's headlights vanished. All I could see was a dark, dark velvet blue nothing and the car horn blast was replaced by a sound like a rushing, roaring water-fall. I felt myself falling backwards and waited to hit the ground – but I never did.

I just kept falling and falling.

Eight

'Heather . . . ?'

I opened my eyes. Andrew's face was so close to mine, I could feel his warm breath on my face. He was staring at me, his eyes wide, an intense, frightened look on his face. Behind him, I could see a couple of other people watching me, their expressions serious. Only then did I realise I was lying down on the pavement. Embarrassed, I scrambled to my feet.

'Andrew, what happened?' I asked, dusting myself off.

'You stepped into the street. I almost hit you.' A man, in his early twenties with blondish, wavy hair spoke with a strong guttural accent. He was tall, over six feet, with the lightest eyes I'd ever seen. In the evening light, I couldn't tell if they were blue or grey. He was wearing dark jeans and a light blue or green shirt. A pullover lay over his shoulders, the arms knotted under his chin. Behind him was a four-door hatchback car, but I didn't recognise the make. When the other people around saw that I was all right, they started to wander off. I was grateful! Spectators were the last thing I needed.

'You bloody idiot! What d'you think you were doing? If I hadn't pulled you out of the way, Heather . . .'

Until Andrew said my name, I thought he was remonstrating with the man who'd almost knocked me over. I glared at him.

'Thank you so much for your concern,' I said.

Andrew glared at me. He took a deep breath, then another.

'Are you sure you're all right?' he asked at last.

I concentrated on my feet, my legs, my back, my head. 'Positive. I must have blacked out for a second. I've never done that before.' I felt like a complete wimp. How embarrassing! How *feeble*!

'You stupid cow!' Andrew pulled me towards him and hugged me so tight I could hardly breathe. I hugged him back, my hands on his shoulders. Slowly, I felt the muscles beneath my hands slacken and relax.

'Sorry I shouted at you. I thought . . . And then when you turned into dead weight in my arms and I couldn't hold you . . . Sorry . . .' He released me, reluctantly.

'Next time, I'll pay more attention to where I'm going.' I smiled at him.

'And you should do the same, mate.' Furious, Andrew turned on the driver. 'You were driving much too fast.'

'You are absolutely right. It was my fault entirely,' the man agreed immediately. He said to me. 'You are not hurt?'

I shook my head.

'My name is Julius. Julius Keller. You are sure you do not need a doctor?'

'Positive. It was my fault, Mr Keller. I shouldn't have stepped out like that. I forgot cars drive on the wrong side of the road on the continent.'

'Call me Julius. You must be British,' he laughed. 'We prefer to call it the *other* side of the road to the practise in Britain, rather than the wrong side.'

I nodded, acknowledging the correction. How could I have said the wrong side? I knew better than that!

'Now then, you must both allow me to make it up to you.' Julius smiled.

'There's no need for that,' said Andrew, still scowling. 'Bloody Italian drivers!' he muttered under his breath.

He's not Italian. Not with that peculiar accent, I thought.

Julius raised a hand. 'I insist. I was travelling much too fast for this road, so you must at least allow me to provide you both with dinner. Have you eaten?'

'Not yet. We've only just dropped off our stuff at the youth hostel. But really, there's no need . . .' I began.

'Please. Let me. I feel terrible about what happened. You must allow me to do this small thing. *Please.*'

I shrugged. Andrew and I exchanged a look. 'Fine with me,' I said.

'Okay, Julius. Thanks,' said Andrew. 'This is Heather and I'm Andrew. Actually, we were wondering where would be a cheap and cheerful place to eat around here . . .'

'I have something even better in mind,' Julius grinned. 'I am having a party for some friends tonight at my house. There will be good music and plenty of food. You will come as my guests.'

'Oh, but we couldn't do that,' I protested. 'We don't want to intrude.'

'It will be no intrusion, I assure you. I would like both of you to come – very much.' A few friends from the youth hostel are already at my house. You may know them? Christine and Scott are from Australia, Carlos and Juan are brothers from Spain . . .'

''Fraid not. We only arrived in Fipoli today so we don't really know anyone yet,' I said.

It was highly unlikely that we would've known them, even if we had been at the hostel longer. There was no way we could get acquainted with everyone there. People came and went so quickly.

'This will be your chance then,' smiled Julius. 'My parties are very friendly. You will be most welcome.'

'I don't know . . .' Andrew frowned. 'I'm not being funny or anything, but we don't really know you.'

'This is true,' Julius nodded, his expression serious. 'But at the youth hostel they know of me and my brother. If you were to ask about me I am sure they would reassure you. And you will enjoy yourself at my party.'

'Heather?' Andrew asked, doubtfully.

'Yeah. Why not?' I smiled.

It sounded fine by me. I hadn't been to a good rave in ages. Mind you, Julius' idea of good music and mine might be worlds apart!

'All right, then,' Andrew agreed at last.

Julius glanced down at his watch. 'My house is about ten minutes drive from here. We will go there together. I will drive.'

'If you're having a party, why aren't you at it?' I frowned.

'I had to take a friend home who did not feel very well and who was not able to drive himself home,' Julius smiled. 'I did not want any of my guests to be inconvenienced, so I took Daniel myself. To tell you the truth, I do not think that many of my friends will have even noticed my absence.'

The mini-cab service in Fipoli was obviously as bad as that back home in Catford!

'You haven't been drinking, have you?' I asked suspiciously. No way was I going to let myself be driven anywhere by someone who'd been drinking.

'No. I do not drink and drive, and I will have to drive some of my friends back to the youth hostel later,' he said.

He walked over to his car and opened the right-hand door. I was puzzled until I remembered that the steering wheels on continental cars were on the left-hand side. I got in and he shut the door behind me. Andrew got in the back. Julius walked around the car to get behind the wheel.

'Julius, what about your parents? Won't they mind you inviting strangers to your house?' Andrew asked.

'I live with my brother and he is away at present. My mother and father are both dead.'

'I'm sorry,' I said sincerely.

'They died a long time ago.'

The way he spoke of his parents, he might have been talking about last week's weather. My dad died when I was ten and I still couldn't string five consecutive sentences together about him without choking up.

But if Julius' parents died when he was a baby, or very young, then maybe that would explain his attitude, I decided. Maybe he couldn't remember a thing about them. My trouble was, I could remember everything about Dad. I kept waiting for the memories to fade but they never did.

On the way to Julius' house, we talked about our holiday so far. I looked at the houses we passed as Andrew and Julius chatted. I wanted to remember the route, just in case we didn't get a lift back to the hostel. It was easy to remember, even for me, and I had absolutely no sense of direction. Julius drove straight along the main street and turned right at the bakery, then he drove up a winding street for about another five minutes. The houses in this street were all terraced, with brightly painted shutters and whitewashed walls. He pulled up outside the last house on the left-hand side of the street. All the lights were on and I could hear the people at the party laughing and music blasting out. I turned and grinned at Andrew.

'The front door is open. Everyone is in the large room to the right, at the top of the stairs. The food is up there also,' said Julius.

'Aren't you coming in?' I asked, surprised.

'As soon as I have parked my car off the road.'

Andrew and I got out of the car. Some music I didn't recognise boomed out into the night air. I wondered how Fipoli neighbours compared to London neighbours!

Andrew said, as we walked towards the front door, 'Heather, are you sure you want to do this?'

'We're here now.' I frowned at him. 'You don't sound very keen. What's the matter?'

'I had other plans for tonight.' He stopped walking and smiled at me. A slow flame crept into my cheeks.

'Oh!' I couldn't think of anything else to say. Andrew's smile broadened. My face was on fire.

'You!' I laughed. 'Well, we don't have to stay too long. An hour at the most?'

'Make it half an hour and it's a deal. I don't want to waste my energy dancing.'

'Andrew, behave!'

'Are you nervous?' he asked gently.

I shook my head. 'To tell the truth, no. Not so much any more. And I want to be with you.'

'Good. 'Cause I want you too.' Andrew bent his head to whisper. 'I'm getting turned on just thinking about you! I love you, Heather.'

'I love you too, Andrew.' My arm crept further around his waist, his arm around my shoulders pulled me even closer.

We entered the house. There were at least four couples kissing on the stairs who didn't even look up when we entered the house. From the laughter and chatter, at least fifty people must be crammed in dancing above us.

'Half an hour,' Andrew said firmly.

'Half an hour,' I agreed.

We went upstairs. At the top of the stairs, there were two doors, one to our left and one to the right. The left-hand door was shut, the right one wide open. It looked like I'd underestimated the number of people. To my surprise a Bob Marley track started. Maybe the party wouldn't be so bad after all! We walked into the room where it was all happening.

A wave of heat and the smell of drink spilled out to meet us. It was so forceful I almost took a step back. It seemed like every light in the entire house had been brought into this one room. White peoples' parties never ceased to amaze me. I preferred parties with every light OUT!

'*Ciao! Come state?*' A pretty girl with straight, dark hair down to her shoulders spoke to us. She was doing a very peculiar dance.

It took a few moments for my brain to switch from English to the few words of Italian at my disposal.

'*Bene, grazie,*' I said, wondering if I'd got even that right! Then I decided to push it. '*Mi chiamo Heather,*' I said.

'Luisa,' she replied. She looked at Andrew.

'And this is Andrew,' I smiled, my Italian defeated.

'Ah! American,' she said.

'No, English,' replied Andrew.

We pushed on into the crowd. All of a sudden, there was an arm around my shoulder, and it wasn't Andrew's. I turned my head. It was Julius.

'I will get you both a drink, yes?' He smiled. 'Wait here. I will bring you the speciality of the house.' And off he went. Andrew turned me round to face him.

'My dance, I believe.' He smiled. And we cuddled up close and swayed to the music. Andrew pulled me even closer to him as we started getting into it. I could tell he was getting excited.

'Fifteen minutes,' he murmured in my ear. I laughed, just about to answer when Julius came back.

'Here we are.' He thrust two long glasses filled with red liquid towards us. I took a glass.

'What is it?' I asked, swirling the liquid around.

'Taste it,' Julius said, mysteriously.

I put it to my lips and sipped tentatively. It was ice cold and tasted sharp and extremely sweet all at the same time. I wasn't too keen.

'It's not bad,' said Andrew, surprised. 'What is it?'

'My secret,' said Julius. And he turned and faded into the crowd.

'D'you want mine?' I whispered.

'Don't you like it?'

'Let me put it this way, if we were next to a house plant, my glass would be empty by now.'

Andrew laughed. He carried on sipping his drink. No sooner was his glass empty than I swapped my half-filled glass for his. He'd just taken his last swig from that, when Julius appeared with two more filled glasses of the same red drink.

'I thought you would both like it,' Julius smiled.

'Yeah, it's all right,' Andrew said.

'It is an acquired taste,' Julius told me. He took our empty glasses after giving us the filled ones. It wasn't a taste I particularly wanted to acquire. I didn't like alcohol much.

For the next hour, Andrew and I danced and laughed with some of the others present. It was good fun, better than either of us had expected. But after about an hour and a half, the strangest feeling came over me. I didn't realise what was going on until I was dancing with Andrew and he had to practically hold me up.

'I think Julius' drink has hit my legs,' I blinked, surprised.

'I feel a bit queasy myself. Maybe what we both need is some fresh air. We should be getting back to the hostel, anyway.'

The crowd had started to thin out by now. We walked out of the room but as soon as I stepped down onto the first stair, my legs went completely.

'I think you had better take Heather to the room of

my brother.' Julius appeared from nowhere to point to the room opposite the one which had held the party.

'Just for five minutes,' I said. 'I just need to sit down for five minutes.'

Julius and Andrew helped me to my feet and into the other bedroom. I couldn't understand it. My brain was functioning, it's just that my legs weren't. One drink and I was plastered. How totally feeble! I didn't usually drink any alcohol at all, and I certainly hadn't had as much of the stuff as Andrew. I'd always thought that people who drank until they were pie-eyed were total dorks. I'd previously always stopped well before my limit, but Julius' drink had sneaked up on me. What *had* he put in it?

So now I was drunk. Was this how it was? Being too blitzed to walk but not too blitzed to know you were blitzed! Another first. This holiday was turning into a whole series of firsts.

I sat down on the bed but once my bum got comfortable, the rest of my body wanted to follow suit. I lay down. And once I closed my eyes, I was out.

Nine

When I awoke, it took me a good minute to remember where I was. I turned my pounding head slowly. Andrew wasn't there. The house was deathly quiet. The party must have finished. It took me another minute to get my legs to work. What *was* in those drinks Julius had brought us? I felt totally grungy, like cold leftovers.

Furious with myself, I tried to call for Andrew, but my voice had gone. There was nothing there. My lips moved but no sound came out. Staggering to my feet, I fell away from the bed to the door. I just wished my head would stop pounding, then I could throw up without worrying about what the noise would do to my head. Never again! I reeled out on to the landing and headed for the room which had held the party. I pushed open the door.

There was Julius, squatting over Andrew's prone body. Andrew was lying half on his back, half on his side facing me, his eyes closed. He looked like he was sleeping. Julius' face had a wax-like pallor and his eyes shone like rubies.

But the thing that made my heart lurch, then almost stop completely was that Julius was holding Andrew's wrist to his mouth. Blood was running over Julius' lips, painting them like garish lipstick.

Julius looked up and we both froze like images in a photograph. I stared unbelieving as blood trickled down from his lips and over his chin. Slowly he wiped his mouth with his free hand. The blood smeared across his face. My mind started screaming, over and over.

No . . . No . . . I opened my mouth. Not a sound came out. I closed my lips. The words erupted.

'NO! G-get away from him.' The sound of Andrew's blood drip-dripping on to the wooden floor finally galvanised me into moving. My voice came back, croaky and hoarse. I flung myself at Julius, battering at him with my fists. He stood up, warding off my blows like swatting away harmless flies.

'What're you doing? Don't. DON'T . . .' I screamed at him.

My mouth filled with cool saliva and my head was whirling. The whole room was spinning wildly. Julius pushed me away. I fell backwards. My head snapped back against the wall and I crumpled up like wet newspaper. My upper body lay against the wall, so limp and sluggish that it must surely fall through it. Julius squatted down and again raised Andrew's wrist to his lips. He was crazy. Totally mad. But how to stop a madman?

'Please . . .' I whispered. Even to my ears my voice sounded ineffectual, weak as dishwater. 'Please, don't hurt him. Andrew and me, we love each other. W-we don't have a-anyone else. Please . . . I'm begging you . . . please don't . . .'

For countless moments, Julius and I watched each other.

'It's too late.' Julius' voice was the merest sigh.

Too late . . . ? My whole body trembled violently. I still couldn't get up.

Do something . . . Anything . . . Stop him . . .
Andrew . . .

'Please . . . I don't have anyone else,' I breathed desperately. 'I love him. Please.' I swallowed hard and tried to continue. 'Let us go. W-we won't tell . . .'

I tried to say more but nothing else would come out.

'Please . . .' I mouthed.

An eternity passed as Julius and I fought silently over

Andrew. A fight with no words and no actions. Then it seemed as if Julius' whole body sagged with defeat. He released Andrew's arm and it fell, hitting heavily against the floor. Slowly, deliberately, his eyes never leaving mine, Julius bit into his own wrist.

My stomach turned somersaults. I swallowed hard and kept on swallowing. If only I could clear my head. If only I could move, do something. But the link between my mind and body had been severed. I watched the blood run from Julius' self-inflicted wound. Against my will, my eyelids closed and I couldn't open them. They weighed a ton each.

Don't hurt him . . . don't hurt him . . . I begged silently. If I could just open my damned eyes. What was Julius doing now? He was sick. A psycho. Crazy. Drinking Andrew's blood like it was water. Biting his own wrist . . . He was demented.

Don't hurt him . . .

Don't pass out, Heather, I told myself urgently. But even as the thought entered my head I knew it was too late. I felt my head fall to one side and the rest of my body went with it.

I've failed you, Andrew, I thought with utter misery. I've failed you. And I'm next.

'Heather? Heather, wake up.'

I struggled to open my eyes.

'Andrew? Andrew!'

'Shush!'

He looked so strange. Pale, almost paper-white and with wide, staring eyes, and flushed-red lips.

'Are you all right? Where's Julius? He's mad. Did he hurt you? I thought he was going to kill you for sure, then me.' I didn't have a clue what I was whispering. It all came out as garbled nonsense to my ears.

58

'Come on, Heather. We've got to get out of here before he comes back. He might change his mind.'

I hardly heard him. 'Change his mind? I don't understand. Where is he?'

'Don't know. Don't care. Let's get out of here!'

With Andrew's help, I clambered to my feet. I took a long, hard look at Andrew.

'Andrew, you look like shit.'

'Thanks.'

Then I remembered. Terrifying thoughts whipped through my head. I looked down at my wrists. No blood. No marks. I pulled Andrew's wrists towards me and scrutinised them. Once again, my heart stopped.

'I wasn't dreaming, then,' I whispered.

The look in his eyes as well as the yellow-blue bruises around the puncture marks on his wrist gave me the answer.

'He's warped. We must go to the police,' I raged. The words, furiously spoken, set my head ringing again. The pneumatic drill was gone but Big Ben had arrived in its stead.

'We can't.' Andrew helped me to the door. My legs still weren't my own.

'Why not?'

'Look, Heather, neither of us is in a fit state to make sense of any of this at the moment, let alone explain it to someone else. Let's go back to the hostel.'

'Shouldn't you at least go to a hospital?' I asked.

Andrew shook his head. 'I only lost a little blood. He didn't do anything else to me.'

'But he might try it on someone else. He might *kill* someone. He might have killed s-someone already . . .'

'He won't do anything else tonight. We'll sort it out tomorrow.'

We were finally down the stairs and heading out the front door.

'How can you be so sure?' My head was full of bells pealing out like there was a royal wedding going on. I leaned heavily on Andrew, my head swimming.

'I feel like death,' I groaned, holding my head.

'It was the drinks Julius gave us. They were spiked.'

'Spiked?' So he could get both of us, I realised. 'Andrew, we *have* to go to the police.'

'No, Heather. Trust me.'

I tilted my head to look at him. 'H-how come you're so . . . calm about all this? Julius is d-dangerous. He might have killed us.'

'But you stopped him.'

'*I* did? But . . .' The rushing, roaring waterfall was back, the sound crashing through my head. With a start, I realised it was the sound of my own blood thundering in my ears.

I almost fell over when Andrew started waving his arms about, my support gone. I was slipping away again.

I vaguely remember being unceremoniously bundled into what I presumed was a taxi. I have no idea how long we drove for, but at some stage I was unceremoniously bundled out again. By this time, if it hadn't been for Andrew's arm around my waist, I would have hit the pavement for sure.

'What was *in* those drinks?' I muttered.

'You don't want to know.'

'D'you know?'

'Yeah. Julius told me. I wish . . . I wish he hadn't,' breathed Andrew.

'He *told* you?' My voice was getting fainter and fainter. 'Did he . . . did he spike anyone else's drink at the p-party?' We made our way into the hostel.

'No, just ours.'

'Andrew, I feel sick.'

'Hang on. All you need is some sleep.'

'We should go to the police. Right now. Right . . .'

'We can't, Heather.'

'Why . . . why not?'

'I'll explain tomorrow. You're in no fit state to understand tonight.'

'But you're all right?' I asked, anxiously.

'Am I all right? That's an interesting question.' Andrew laughed, a harsh, grating laugh that was totally unfamiliar. Totally unlike his normal laugh.

Even in my semi-unconscious state, I could detect the bitterness in his voice. Bitterness and something else. Something I couldn't quite place. Fear? From far away, I heard Andrew explain to Marcus the receptionist that I didn't feel well. The understatement of the decade.

'Just a little further, Heather.' Andrew's voice was retreating all the time.

We were in our room. I fell away from him onto the nearest bed.

'We should go to the police. I'll go. I'll . . . see them. Right . . . this. . . .' I tried to stand up and failed miserably. I looked up at Andrew. He was watching me, with a look on his face I'd never seen before.

'Andrew, w-what's going on? I feel so . . . peculiar.'

'You'll be all right. I love you, Heather.'

'I . . . I know,' I whispered. My head rocked back. My eyes closed.

And once again, I checked out.

When I woke up, I was alone. The moment I opened my eyes I knew that Andrew was no longer in the room with me. Groaning against the headache that threatened to split my skull wide open, I looked towards the window. The thin, faded cotton curtains were still drawn but daylight filtered past them and through them, speckling the room with white light.

I wondered where he was. Was he all right? Our first

61

stop this morning would be the nearest police station, that was for sure. I noticed that Andrew's bed was made. It looked like it hadn't even been slept in. Past his bed there was only one back pack – mine. A sheet of A4 paper sat self-consciously on his pillow. I sat up. Wincing again as my head threatened to drop off, I half wished it would to put me out of my misery. Lurching between the beds, I grabbed the sheet of paper and sat down gingerly. No sudden movements and maybe my head would forgive me for guzzling alcohol. Never, *ever* again. Andrew said the drinks were spiked . . . Or had I dreamt that bit?

> *Darling Heather,*
> *For reasons I'll explain when I see you, I've had to go home, back to London. I promise I'm fine so don't worry, but follow me straight home. Don't talk to anyone and on NO account go to the police. It's very important that you don't let me down.*
> *I love you.*
> *Andrew.*

I read the letter again and a third time. With each passing moment, I knew for certain that my head was going to explode, but not from a hangover, from rage.

He'd actually left me here and buggered off home without me. I read the letter a fourth time and *still* couldn't believe it. How could he? Why did he?

'Bastard . . . BASTARD!'

I crumpled up the letter and threw it against the wall.

'You bastard, Andrew,' I muttered, holding my head. 'You just wait 'til I see you.'

Ten

I was tempted to go to the police anyway, in spite of Andrew's wishes. Reluctantly I retrieved Andrew's letter, straightened it out and read it again. Why was he so insistent that I *shouldn't* go to the police? It didn't make any sense. What was he playing at? Why had he left me alone here? When did he leave? Questions and more questions buzzed around my mind like angry wasps.

I couldn't believe it. It had to be a joke. Andrew wouldn't really leave me alone and go home without me? Looking around my small room, I knew I was only fooling myself. The room was still, silent. From another room I heard a cough. It made me feel even more isolated. I'd never felt so lonely. So alone.

He really had gone. Andrew really had gone and left me here. But why? I bit down on my bottom lip. No reason in the world would be good enough to explain why he'd done it. It was almost as though he'd run away. But from what? From me?

I couldn't understand it. Andrew was safe. We'd been stupid and careless to let Julius get to us like that, but we'd escaped. So what was this all about?

With a cry of exasperation, I sprung off the bed. I'd had enough. All I wanted to do now was go home. Julius was someone else's problem. I wanted to get as far away from him and Fipoli and the whole damned country as I could get. Julius was obviously several trains short of a full service. He probably drugged people, then drank some of their blood and then let them go. After all, he'd let us go. Andrew had said something about leaving Julius' house before he changed his mind – so he *must* have let us go. Yeah, Julius was definitely someone else's problem. I had more important things on my mind. Like getting home. We were both okay. I was alive. So was Andrew.

But he wouldn't be once I caught up with him!

Four days later I was back in England. Four whole days it took me. And with each passing moment, the rage inside me intensified until I was choking on it. The week's events had assumed an unreal, dreamlike quality. As I got further and further away from Fipoli, both in distance and in time, I wasn't sure which of my memories were real and which ones were the result of too many spiked drinks or too much imagination. The part where I'd pleaded for Andrew's life for example. Was that real?

One thing was certain, Andrew had dumped me. After four days of thinking about practically nothing else, I was sure that was what it was all about. He'd dumped me after my paralytic newt display and was too much of a coward to tell me so.

I told myself I was being stupid. Why would someone who had professed to love me be put off by my falling unconscious. I hadn't done it on purpose, after all. But I couldn't get past the conclusion that I'd definitely been dumped. What other explanation was there?

After all, it wasn't as if it hadn't happened before. Dad had said he loved us too, but it hadn't stopped him from leaving.

There were no two ways about it. Andrew had left me stranded. He'd gone back home, leaving me in Fipoli to fend for myself. I'd never forgive him for that, never. I burned to see him, to tell him how much I despised him.

And I so needed to see him, to see whether the conclusion I'd reached was true or false. If it was true that he'd dumped me, I wouldn't show him how much it hurt. I was good at that. I wouldn't hear him laughing because I'd laugh first and loudest.

As the ferry reached England, I found myself hating Andrew. Really hating him. I'd got through the lonely train rides across Europe, the waiting in empty stations, the restless overnight stays in hostels we'd not previously planned to stop at, the meals alone, the pitying looks – I'd got through them all, just by thinking about what I'd do when I caught up with Andrew.

The train crawled from the coast to central London – frustrating to say the least. There seemed to be points and signal failures about every half mile, and by the time I eventually reached home it was dark.

'Mum!' I shouted as soon as I stepped through the door.

Silence. Then I remembered that Mum and Jessica were in Ireland and wouldn't be back for another week. How I wished they were at home, or that I'd gone with them. This permanent concrete block sitting in my chest really wasn't worth it. Andrew wasn't worth it. *Bastard!*

I longed for someone to talk to. I'd even have settled for Jessica. When that thought entered my head, I knew I was in a bad way. Fighting against the self-pity I felt, I dropped my back pack in the hall before straightening up slowly. I breathed deeply.

Home.

For the first time since I went on holiday, I realised just how much I'd missed it. Faint traces of Mum's herb dumplings and air freshener and her perfume hung in the air. I was so weary I just wanted to go to bed and curl up and not move until Mum and Jessica came home, but I had things to do. Mentally rolling up my sleeves, I opened our front door and stepped out into the night again. Alternating between running and walking, I headed for Andrew's house. I didn't phone him first to warn him that I was about to descend. Some things are better done face to face.

At last I reached my destination. And by the time I' did, I was so full of rage my hands kept clenching and unclenching. I was tempted to keep my finger on the door bell until the front door opened, but then Mrs Harrison might open the door instead of Andrew. I didn't want to waste even the smallest smidgen of anger on her. I rang the bell. Almost immediately the front door opened. I mentally grimaced. It was Mr Harrison. When he saw me, his eyes opened wide.

'Hello, Heather,' he said, surprised.

'Hi, Mr Harrison. Is Andrew at home? Can I speak to him please?'

'I don't understand.' Mr Harrison stared at me. 'Isn't he with you? We weren't expecting you back until next week.'

'Frederick, who is it?' Mrs Harrison emerged from her pristine, designer kitchen. 'Oh, it's you.'

'Susan, Heather's asking for Andrew.'

'Andrew?' she said sharply. 'He's with you.'

In the silence that followed I could actually hear my heartbeat speed up.

'I . . . I . . .' At the look of dawning anxiety on Mrs Harrison's face I couldn't think of anything to say.

'Where's my son?' Mrs Harrison strode to the front door, sweeping Mr Harrison aside.

'Andrew left me alone in Fipoli,' I explained quickly. 'He left me a note saying he'd meet me at home . . .'

'Andrew would never do that,' she interrupted angrily.

'I'm not lying. That's exactly what he did,' I replied, just as angry as she was. 'I have the note he left me if you don't believe me.'

'Show me,' demanded Mrs Harrison.

'Now then, Susan, let's all just calm down shall we?' Mr Harrison soothed.

I searched through the pockets of my jeans for Andrew's letter, before I remembered where it was.

'I've left it in my back pack at home,' I mumbled, annoyed, adding in a louder voice, 'But he *did* leave me. He said he'd explain why when I got back home.'

'He's not here, Heather,' Mr Harrison frowned. 'We haven't seen him since the two of you went on holiday together.' His voice held the faintest recriminatory hint which I chose to ignore.

'Did you two have a quarrel? Is that why Andrew isn't home yet?' Mrs Harrison's glaring dislike for me was so forceful that I took an involuntary step backwards.

'No, we didn't quarrel,' I said indignantly.

'Susan, calm down.' Mr Harrison placed a restraining hand on his wife's arm. 'I'm sure there's a perfectly reasonable, rational explanation why Andrew came home without Heather.'

'We only have her word for that.'

'Are you calling me a liar?' I flared up.

'No, Heather, my wife isn't accusing you of any such thing. Are you dear?' Mr Harrison said firmly. 'We're just worried that's all. You say that Andrew left Fipoli before you?'

'That's what he said in his letter,' I replied slowly, fighting to control my temper. I hated being called a liar. 'He said he'd see me at home so I assumed he was coming straight here.'

'Where is he now then?' Mrs Harrison asked.

If I knew that I wouldn't be wasting my time with you, I thought.

From the way her eyes narrowed I could tell she'd

deciphered those thoughts. I lowered my gaze immediately.

'I'll go to the Burger Bar. Maybe he's there, or someone there has seen him.'

'If you find him tell him to come straight home will you?' Mr Harrison said. I nodded and turned away from them.

'Heather Lucas, if anything's happened to my son I'll never forgive you,' Mrs Harrison said from behind me.

'Susan!' Mr Harrison admonished.

I turned around again to look at them.

'Frederick, something has happened to Andrew. I can feel it,' Mrs Harrison protested.

'Andrew's fine, Mrs Harrison, I just know he is,' I said.

I'm the one who got left behind, after all. I'm the one who had to fight my way back to London. I'm the girl who got left on her own. Andrew, you git, just wait 'til I get my hands on you . . .

'Mum, what's she doing here?'

I froze at the sound of Morgan's voice.

'Andrew's not home yet — and she is,' Mrs Harrison replied. 'If Andrew's not home by midnight, I'm going to call the police.'

'Now, Susan, you know how much Andrew hates fuss and bother,' Mr Harrison chided.

'I don't care. My son is missing. She should know where he is, and she doesn't.'

'Where's my brother?' Morgan grabbed my arm, yanking me around to face him.

'If I knew that I wouldn't be round here asking,' I hissed at him, pulling back my arm.

'What the hell's going on?' Morgan frowned.

'Mr Harrison,' I addressed myself to the most reasonable of the Harrison clan. 'I'll go to the Burger Bar and see if he's there.'

Andrew, thank you so much for leaving me to face your family all by myself. I wouldn't wish that on my worst enemy, I thought sourly.

With the thoughts racing around my mind, I was surprised the air around my head wasn't a deep shade of blue.

Giving Morgan a wide berth, I walked past their open gate and began to walk up the road.

'I'll be right back, Dad,' I heard Morgan say from behind me.

I walked faster. I heard Morgan's heavy feet pounding behind me. Perspiration trickled down my back like rain down a window pane. He ran in front of me, barring my way.

'I want to talk to you,' he said stonily.

'Shift, Morgan. I'm not in the mood for you. Not tonight.' I tried to walk around him but he stepped in front of me, blocking my way again.

'Oh no you don't.' Morgan's smile sent a chill down my spine. 'I want to talk to you, and this time Andrew isn't here to stop me.'

Eleven

'You're in my way, Morgan.'

My heart was hammering so loudly I wondered if he could hear it. Morgan regarded me, his expression hard as granite.

'Where's my brother?' he said at last.

'I don't know. That's what I'm trying to find out,' I said slowly with deliberate patience.

'If anything's happened to him . . .'

Anger flared through my body.

'Look, your brother left me in Fipoli and came home without me, *not* the other way around. Doesn't anyone in your family give a monkey's about anyone but themselves?'

'You're here, my brother isn't.'

I breathed deeply. 'I'm going to the Burger Bar and then I'm going home. And if I *do* see your brother then I'll have a few things to say to him myself. I've had more than enough of your family to last me a lifetime.'

'I'm coming with you,' Morgan said.

'You are not.'

'I'm coming with you whether you like it or not. Don't run away with the idea that I want your company.'

Stretching out my fingers, I stepped past him and carried on walking. This time he didn't stop me but fell into step beside me. I walked so quickly that by the time we reached the Burger Bar I was out of breath. Pete and Vijay were the only two from our usual gang in there.

'Why, hello Heather. I thought you'd still be on holiday,' Pete said.

'I came back today.' I forced myself to smile at him. 'I don't suppose you've seen Andrew?'

'Not since before you went on holiday together,' Pete said, looking from me to Morgan and back again. 'Why d'you ask?'

'I just thought he might be in here.' I shrugged.

Pete looked at Vijay before shaking his head.

'Where are you off to now?' Pete asked, at the same time regarding Morgan with animosity.

'Home.'

'Want me to come with you?'

Conscious of Morgan tensing beside me, I said, 'Would you? That's very kind of you.' I'd been dreading leaving the restaurant with only Morgan for company.

'No problem.' Pete glanced at his watch, before standing up. 'I'll see you tomorrow, Vijay.'

I risked a glance at Morgan. He was scowling at me.

'Something wrong?' I asked.

'You'd better pray that Andrew turns up soon,' Morgan said quietly. He turned around and marched out of the Burger Bar.

'He's a real charmer, isn't he?' Pete said quietly from beside me.

'Not quite the word I had in mind,' I said. We left the Burger Bar in silence.

'So what's going on?' Pete said at last. 'Anything you want to tell me about?'

I smiled at him, grateful as never before for Pete's friendship. I couldn't help wondering what it would've been like to go out with him rather than with Andrew.

Ten months ago Andrew and I had been standing separately outside the local cinema and the main feature had already started. It was obvious we'd both been stood up. It was bucketing down and a chill wind

71

whistled around me, but I was *boiling*. I glared at Andrew as if it was his fault, daring him to say a word. He might be used to his dates not turning up, but I certainly wasn't. My first so-called date with Pete Shorman was definitely going to be my last. With a face like a handful of mince I was just about to march home when Andrew sidled up to me.

'You been stood up too?' he grinned.

I glared at him, torn between lying to save my face and flouncing off without a word.

'Brilliant deduction, Einstein.' I turned away.

'Look, Heather, I . . . I've got two tickets to . . . er . . . see this film and it'd really hurt if one of them went to waste. So why don't we . . . we could go in and see . . . see it together.' Andrew stammered in his haste to get the words out.

He must have seen the frown deepening on my face because he continued hastily, 'We wouldn't be on a date or anything. We'd be . . . just two friends watching the same film.'

Who told you we're friends? I thought sourly.

I was livid with Pete so I did something I never thought I'd do.

'I suppose I've nothing better to do this evening,' I shrugged ungraciously. 'All right, then.'

And that was that. We went in to see the film together, and it turned out to be very good indeed. Andrew and I wandered into a pizza place afterwards – only because we were both hungry – and discussed the film, moving on to other films we'd seen, books we'd read and who we knew at school. He'd had me in fits of laughter with his screwy sense of humour.

I discovered something strange that night. Andrew was *all right*! Over our pizzas he asked me out to see another film I'd already expressed an interest in. It'd only taken me a couple of seconds to say yes. And the rest, as the saying goes, was history.

I didn't speak to Pete for at least a week, even though he'd tried to fob me off with dry excuses on a couple of occasions. Finally, and thankfully, he had given up.

We were friends now, Pete and I. But I still reckoned that when he knew he couldn't make our date, he should have tried to phone me or, at the very least, have left a message. Leaving me standing outside the cinema like a real lemon had been totally out of order.

Looking up at him now, I couldn't help thinking how strange it was, the way things worked out. Now I was *almost* sorry Pete did stand me up. All that emotional energy I'd expended on Andrew had probably all been for nothing.

'Come on, Heather, what is it?' Pete took my arm and linked it with his own. The gesture was oddly comforting. 'You look as if you could use a friend.'

I chewed on my bottom lip.

'It's Andrew. He left Fipoli and came home without me. The trouble is no one seems to have seen him since. I'm beginning to get worried. And of course his family are blaming me, although it was Andrew who did the bunk, not the other way around.'

'So what happened between the two of you in Fipoli?' Pete frowned.

'Nothing. That's just it. We were having a great time, until the party.'

'The party?' Pete prompted.

I looked up at him, then quickly looked away. 'Nothing. It's not important. Right now all I want to do is find Andrew.'

Abruptly I stopped speaking. Without warning the hairs on my nape had started to prickle. I turned my head and looked down the street. There was no one there.

73

'What's the matter?' Pete asked, looking down the street with me.

'I don't know. I'm not sure.' I rubbed the back of my neck but the prickling refused to go away. 'Let go, Pete.'

The prickling at my nape turned to a burning. I turned sharply. Something was wrong. I could feel it.

Twelve

I looked up and down the street. The road was empty.

'Heather, what are you doing?' Pete asked.

'Nothing. Sorry Pete. I guess I'm just tired.' I forced a smile and walked faster.

'I'm sure Andrew will turn up,' Pete smiled, mistaking the reason for my tension.

'I hope so.'

'I *know* so,' Pete replied. 'Now then, I want to know all about your holiday. Where did you go and what did you do?'

For the remaining ten minutes until I reached home, I told Pete about the places Andrew and I had visited in the first week and a bit of our holiday. But talking about him just made me more angry and even more sad until in the end I was choking up, so I had to stop.

We reached my front gate.

'Will you be okay, Heather?'

'Of course. I'll get some sleep. That's all I need now,' I said, rubbing the back of my neck.

'Yeah, I can see you're tired.' Pete smiled. 'Look, if you need me for anything – anything at all – just phone.'

'I'll take you up on that. Thanks, Pete.'

On impulse I stretched up and kissed his cheek.

'Thanks again, Pete,' I said, embarrassed.

'Look after yourself, Heather.' Pete turned and walked away from me. I watched him until he turned the corner, then with a sigh I opened the gate and walked to my front door. I was cold. After searching through all my jacket pockets, I finally found my front door keys. I walked into the house. Chilled, I turned back to look at the empty street. The lights from the houses opposite made me feel even more alone. Mum and Jessica were in Ireland, and how I wished they weren't.

'Oh Andrew, where are you? I wish you were here... right here. Right now. You swine!'

A strong, icy wind blew past me and into the hall. I shivered and shut the front door. The silence in the house was almost eerie. A strange kind of listening silence.

Wearily I climbed the stairs to my bedroom, not bothering to turn on the hall light as I went. I trudged to my bedroom, ready to fall on my bed, exhausted from travelling and anger and disappointment and worry. I put my hand out to turn on the light switch when someone grabbed my wrist. I opened my mouth to scream blue murder.

'Heather, Heather don't. It's me...'

'Andrew?' I peered through the darkness. All I could see was his outline. 'Andrew, that is you, isn't it?'

'Who else would it be? Pete?'

The relief I felt vanished immediately. Andrew's voice sounded strange, hard. Sort of hollow.

'Leave Pete out of this,' I said furiously. 'Where the hell have you been? Why did you leave me alone in Fipoli? How dare you? How *could* you?'

Once again my hand moved towards the light switch.

'No, Heather. Don't put it on. Not yet.'

'Why not? I want to see you. I bet you look just great. Meanwhile I've been worrying myself sick. I hate you for what you put me through. Hate you, hate you. Listen to me! You've turned me into a damned nagging fishwife. That's something else I can thank you for! I sound like my mother.'

'I didn't want to leave you alone but I had no choice.'

76

'What d'you mean?' I stormed. 'Let's hear your excuse then, and it'd better be ace.'

Andrew looked weird in the darkness. Just a hazy outline that wouldn't keep still, moving restlessly around the room.

'Heather, I . . . I'm different now. I look different . . .' He was a silhouette against my bedroom window. If the curtains had been drawn or the moon new, I wouldn't have been able to see a thing.

'What do you mean – different? Look, I've had enough of this.'

Andrew's hand was on mine the moment after I had switched on the light. I only had time to register that much before he turned quickly so that his back was towards me. I blinked at him stupidly. How had he made it across my bedroom so quickly? I hadn't even heard him move. He was dressed in dark green jeans and the cream cotton sweater his mum knitted for him. He didn't have that outfit when we went on holiday.

'So you *have* been home?' I said, puzzled. 'I don't understand. I've just come from your place. Your mum was on my case because she hasn't seen you.'

'I was there earlier. I changed my clothes but made sure no one saw me.'

'Why? Your family all think I've murdered you and left your body in Fipoli.'

'I . . . I wanted you to see me first, Heather.' Andrew said slowly.

'I don't understand. And . . . wait a minute, how did you get in here? All the doors and windows are locked.'

There was a pause.

'I got past you when you opened your front door,' Andrew replied at last. 'You invited me in.'

'I invited you . . . ? What're you talking about?'

'You wished I was here with you, so I came in.'

77

'But I don't get it. How did you get past me without me seeing you?'

A slow chill ran down my spine. 'Andrew? Look at me. Please.' I walked towards him.

Without warning he turned around to face me. I gasped and stumbled backwards.

Don't Heather, don't, I kept telling myself over and over. It's Andrew. Don't. But I couldn't help it. I screamed.

Thirteen

Andrew's face twisted. 'I told you I looked different.'

'My God . . .'

'It's still me, Heather.' Andrew took a step towards me, his arms outstretched.

Again I stumbled, backing into the bedroom door.

'Heather, don't . . .' Andrew pleaded. 'Now you see why I didn't want anyone to see me before you did.'

I looked at him – I didn't blink once – and still I couldn't believe my eyes. His face was pale, as pale as milk. Even his lips were pale, and thinner than usual.

But it was his eyes . . .

They were no longer the warm jade green I remembered. They were hard and cold, like clear, green glass. It was like looking into the eyes of a stranger.

'Andrew? W-what's going on?' I whispered.

There was a long pause. I wanted him to rush towards me. To hug me and tell me that everything was okay, that nothing had changed between us, that he *was* the same as ever.

But he didn't.

'Let me see your wrists,' I ordered.

Andrew held out his hands, palms up. I took them in my own. They were cool, almost cold. I bent my head for a closer look.

There were two faint marks on his wrist, about three centimetres apart. If I hadn't been looking for the marks, I'd never have noticed them.

'So I wasn't dreaming. I wasn't sure . . .'

'The scars have healed.' The words were spoken so

softly I almost didn't catch them. 'Julius offered me a choice, Heather. Life or death. My decision.'

'I don't understand.'

'He bit me . . . drank my blood.'

'I know. I saw.'

'Heather, you pleaded for my life but you were too late. Julius said he told you that, but you didn't understand. You couldn't understand. You were too late. I'd lost too much blood. When you begged for my life, he felt sorry for me, for both of us . . . for all of us. So he brought me round and offered me life or death. My choice. No one else's. I . . . I chose to live.'

The blood rushing through my head almost drowned out Andrew's words. I wanted to drown out his words. Every single one of them.

'So Julius saved my life . . . by giving me his blood.'

'He bit his wrist,' I breathed. 'I remember.' The full memory came limping back.

'Julius gave me back my life the only way he could.' Andrew took a step towards me. 'He made me drink from him, he made me the same as him.'

'But blood transfusions don't work like that,' I said, confused.

'Heather, I'm not talking about a blood transfusion. I drank Julius' blood. I'm the same as him now. A . . . vampire.'

Silence descended like a shroud around us. Slowly, I began to laugh.

'Yeah, right. Now tell me why you *really* deserted me in Fipoli,' I said, my laughter fading. 'I'll give you ten out of ten for originality though. That's the best cock-and-bull story I've ever heard.'

'It's the truth, Heather,' Andrew said quietly. 'Julius made me a vampire.'

'Yeah, right . . .'

'It's the truth.'

'Where are your fangs then?' I folded my arms across my chest. I couldn't believe I was even indulging Andrew in this ridiculous conversation.

'My canine teeth emerge only when I'm about to feed.'

'Of course they do,' I said. 'Andrew, this isn't funny any more. Are you going to tell me why you dumped me or not?'

'Heather, you're not listening to me.'

'If you don't want to go out with me any more, why can't you just come right out and say it? Why all this phooey? And you could have told me before we went away on . . .'

'HEATHER, SHUT UP!'

Every word in my mouth dried up.

'I'm telling you the truth. Do you think I like this? Don't you think I know how this sounds. But it's what I am now. I can't go back. I can't change it. It was my choice. Heather . . .' Andrew closed his eyes, tilting back his head. The look of utter despair on his face said more than a thousand words. I didn't know how to respond. I didn't know what to think. Then I realised. The drinks Julius had given us. He must have put some kind of hallucinatory drug in them. I'd *thought* I'd seen Julius drinking Andrew's blood. Andrew *thought* he was a vampire. But why was I over my drink, and Andrew still wasn't over his? Perhaps because he'd had more than me. We should both go and get ourselves checked out. The doctors would be able to explain.

'Andrew, I think we should both go to the local hospital. We should see a doctor. Whatever Julius put in our drinks is obviously still in your blood stream. It might still be in mine . . . We need to . . .'

Andrew grabbed my arm and pulled me over to my dressing-table mirror. He stood beside me as I looked into it. I stared and stared until I thought my eyes must surely fall from their sockets. My image was reflected back perfectly normally. Andrew's wasn't. In fact I had to strain to see him. Looking in the mirror, he was a blur. Little more than a mist that I could see right through to the bedroom wall behind us.

'I'm telling the truth.'

My blood turned to ice inside me. I started shaking and once I'd started, I couldn't stop. Both my hands flew to my mouth. I turned to look at him. He was solid, real. I turned back at his reflection. It hadn't changed. Indistinct mist. I backed away, staring at Andrew.

'Are you going to turn away from me?' Andrew asked, his voice the saddest I'd ever heard it.

'No! Come on! This isn't real. You're playing a joke on me, aren't you? God, I'm gullible!' I tried to laugh and failed miserably. He didn't say anything. He didn't have to. I searched for something else to say, but my mind was blank.

'Are you going to turn away from me?' Andrew asked again.

I don't know how long we stood, watching each other. Hours or seconds.

Slowly I walked towards him, trying not even to acknowledge the presence of a mirror in my room. My body was trembling, my heart pumping like a piston. I shook my head.

'I'm not turning away.' I tried to smile but my face twisted in parody. I stopped walking when we were only inches apart. I wanted to reach out, to touch him, but I couldn't. Strange excitement mingled with real and intense fear inside me. I'd never felt so peculiar.

'Tell me what happened,' I said, for want of something better to say.

Where were the important things, the earth-shattering things that I should have been saying? My head was filled with small details. 'What happened when I . . . I passed out?'

'I wasn't feeling too good myself. I lay down next to you for a while until my head wasn't spinning so much. The party had finished by then. I went to ask Julius if he could phone for a taxi for us. I went into his room, I started to ask . . .' Andrew frowned deeply, 'but I don't remember much after that. The rest you know better than I do.'

'But I thought I was out for ages.'

Andrew shook his head. 'If you hadn't woken up, I'd be dead.'

Was that really true? Andrew's expression was serious.

'I didn't say much. I didn't do anything,' I shook my head.

'According to Julius, you said enough.'

'You spoke to him?'

'When he'd revived me with his own blood, yes.'

'I see.' I didn't see at all.

'He explained what I was . . . what to expect.'

I swallowed hard. 'You still haven't told me why you left me alone.' It was important to keep talking. Talking stopped my thoughts from overwhelming me.

'I had to sort out in my own mind what was happening. I had to be alone for a while. And I could only travel at night.'

I hardly heard a word.

We watched each other silently. There were only centimetres between us, yet I couldn't work out if we'd ever been so close together – or so far apart. I opened my mouth to beg Andrew to tell me he was joking. This had to be a joke. But his eyes . . . his eyes told me better than any words that it wasn't. And yet I couldn't take it in. Andrew was a real, live . . .

There were no such things. But here he was . . .

'Are you...do you...drink...like Julius?!' I asked. I had to ask. Surely the truth couldn't be as horrific as the pictures my mind was painting?

'I have to. Otherwise I'll die.'

My mouth opened but snapped shut again without uttering a word. It was impossible to frame my next question.

'Heather, I don't prey on ... people. I feed on animals,' Andrew said quietly.

Was my expression really so easy to read?

'Animals?' I repeated stupidly.

Andrew shrugged. 'Cats, dogs ...'

'Live animals?'

Andrew nodded. 'It has to be fresh, warm blood ...' His sentence trailed off at my very visible shiver of revulsion.

'I have no choice, Heather. Do you want me to die?'

'Of course not. That's not fair,' I protested.

'What are you getting so worked up about? You eat meat. Chickens, lambs, cows ...'

'That's different.'

'How is it different? Because it's cooked?' Andrew mocked.

'Because it's ... it's dead by the time it gets to me,' I replied fiercely.

'So it's all right because you don't do your own killing?'

'Yes ... I ... no, I never said that.' Wearily I moved away from Andrew and sat on my bed. He walked over to me, his eyes never leaving my face. Each of his steps was measured, as if he was giving me every chance to move away from him, or tell him to back off. He sat down on the bed and if he wasn't next to me, then he wasn't exactly at the other end of the bed either.

'I disgust you,' he said.

I couldn't answer. Reaching out I took hold of his hand. It felt icy cold. Even colder than before.

'I . . . You know how much I . . . I love you Andrew.' I took a deep breath. 'Nothing's changed that. You'll just have to give me some time to get used to the idea, that's all. I'm having trouble believing . . . accepting it. When you left me alone in Fipoli I thought . . . I thought that maybe you'd decided we were a mistake. I thought that leaving me alone was the only way you could think of to tell me without a scene.'

'You always did think too much.'

Neither of us spoke for a while.

'How . . . how does it feel? How do you feel?' I asked. 'I can't imagine . . .'

In the silence that followed, I thought Andrew wasn't going to answer my question.

'I'm scared, Heather,' he said suddenly, his eyes fixed on the wall directly in front of me.

'Scared?' I whispered.

'Terrified.' He tried to laugh. 'I feel so . . . Even you shunned me.'

'I didn't. At least . . . I didn't mean to. It was just such a shock.'

I shuffled along the bed to sit next to him, putting my arms around his waist. He placed a hesitant arm around my shoulders.

'I'm here, Andrew.' I didn't know what else to say.

'Heather, I want to ask you something.'

'I'm listening,' I prompted.

Something grave was about to happen. I could feel it. My breath caught in my throat and refused to move any higher. I looked up at Andrew. He looked at me.

'What is it, Andrew?' I asked.

Slowly Andrew stroked my skin, from my earlobe down to where my neck joined my shoulder. His icy fingers sent an electric shiver racing through me. At last he spoke, but I had to strain to catch his words even though I was right next to him.

'Heather,' he said. 'Let me drink from you.'

Fourteen

I didn't even try to pretend that I'd misheard. The only sound in the room was my heart hammering.

'Heather, don't be scared,' Andrew said softly. He looked down at my breast as if he could see my heart through my jumper, through my flesh. 'Let me drink.' His words were mesmerising. 'Then you can be like me. Then we can be together, always. Don't you want us to be together? Please . . .'

'Andrew . . .'

The peal of the doorbell at that moment was like ice water thrown over me.

The spell was broken.

'Don't answer it,' Andrew said, annoyed.

'I have to, Andrew.' I pulled out of his grasp. 'It might be important.'

I bolted out of the room, shutting the door behind me and ran downstairs. Time to think. That's what I needed. What would have happened, what would I have said to Andrew if the doorbell hadn't rang? I flung open the door.

'Oh it's you, Heather. Thank goodness for that.'

'Hi, Mrs Tout,' I said, unable to keep the sigh out of my voice.

'I thought you were away on holiday.' Mrs Tout frowned at me.

'I was. We . . . we came back early.'

'Oh, I see. I knew your mum and sister were in Ireland and I thought you were away, so when I saw the light on in your bedroom, I naturally wondered . . .' She trailed off. I didn't help her out. 'Well, it could have been burglars. I saw your light on . . .'

I could well believe that Mrs Tout had seen my light. Mum and I often joked about our neighbour sitting by her window each evening peering into her neighbours' houses. Mum said it had to be cheaper and more interesting than watching the soaps on telly. Mrs Tout was the typical suburban widow. Pearls and twin-sets were her uniform, the latter always chosen carefully to co-ordinate with her permanent blue rinse. Looking at her, I realised that for the first time I was more grateful for the interruption than irritated by her nosiness.

'Mrs Tout, what would you have done if it had been burglars who opened the door instead of me?' I asked, dryly.

Mrs Tout started at my words. She frowned at me, then slowly smiled.

'I don't know,' she admitted. 'I hadn't got as far as working that part out. I saw the light and marched straight over here.'

'Well, it's only me.' I smiled back.

Neither of us spoke for a few moments.

'So why did you come back from your holiday early?' asked Mrs Tout.

Here we go, I thought, resigning myself to a ten-hour session on the doorstep.

'Heather, who is it?'

Mrs Tout almost jumped out of her shoes at the sound of Andrew's voice from upstairs.

'Who's that?' she asked suspiciously, after regaining her composure.

'Oh, er . . . it's Andrew.'

'Oh, I see.'

She saw far too much! Annoyed and embarrassed, my face grew warm. I wanted to explain that Andrew's presence in the house was perfectly innocent. Then I got even more annoyed and embarrassed at wanting to explain something that was none of Mrs Tout's business. And as for Andrew's presence being innocent . . . He was a . . . !

I couldn't even say it. I couldn't even *think* it. It was horrible. Unreal. Untrue. Here he was, pale and cold and with eyes that gave me ice burns. Yet he was still my Andrew. And I was still crazy about him. So why was my stomach turning and churning at the thought of him?

Behind me, he came slowly down the stairs. Mrs Tout's head craned forward like a tortoise stretching its head out of its shell.

'How's your mother, Andrew?' Mrs Tout said with a frown.

If I hadn't been standing directly in her way, I'm sure she would've pushed past me.

'She's fine thank you,' Andrew said, his tone polite but icy.

'Are you feeling all right, Andrew? You look a little strange.' Mrs Tout's frown deepened.

'I'm fine, Mrs Tout. Never better,' Andrew replied.

I glanced behind. Andrew was half-way down the stairs. The hall light wasn't on, so what little light there was came from the street lamp outside. Andrew's face was partly in shadow, partly illuminated by the dim light outside. He did indeed look strange.

An uneasy silence reigned.

'Well, I'll leave you two to it.' Mrs Tout's blush at her own words was very noticeable. I was tempted to ask her just what it was she thought she was leaving us to.

'Okay, Mrs Tout. Thanks for looking out for our house.'

'You're welcome,' she replied, missing the irony in

my voice. I waved her off, closing the door firmly behind her.

'I knew it was her all the time. I could hear her from up in your bedroom. Nosy old trout!' Andrew said with disgust.

'You're a right one to talk about nosy trouts. I shut my bedroom door, but you still opened it to have a listen.'

'No, I didn't.'

'All right then. You came out on to the landing.'

'Nope. I could hear both of you perfectly well from your bedroom,' he shrugged. 'I reckoned you needed rescuing, that's all.'

'You heard me? With the door shut?' I was sceptical, until the look on Andrew's face told me that he wasn't joking.

'Heather, I can do all sorts of things I'd never even dreamt of before,' he said, walking towards me. He took my hands in his. His hands were even colder now. They felt horrible. Almost clammy. 'I can hear things I could never hear before; conversations from across the street, a dog panting at the top of the road . . . Heather, you'd love it. Let me . . .'

I pulled my hands away from his. 'No . . . not now, Andrew, please. Don't . . . I can't take this in. Not all at once. Please . . .'

'Heather, I don't have much . . .' Andrew raised a paper-white hand to his temples. He swayed slightly.

'What's the matter?' I moved towards him.

'I h-have to go. I'll be back soon.'

He was lurching around like a drunk now. He placed one hand on the wall to steady himself but it didn't do much good. I ran to hold him up.

'Where are you going? What's wrong?'

I don't think he heard me. Andrew pushed past me,

towards the front door. He pulled it open and staggered down the path, leaving the door wide open.

'Andrew . . .' I started after him.

'No! Don't follow me,' he hissed.

Uncertain, I watched him, wondering what I should do.

'I'll be back.' His whisper was harsh and drawn. He ignored me and started off down the street like a bat out of hell. I shut the front door and leaned against it. What now? At least I had some breathing space. I walked into the kitchen and splashed my face under the cold tap. I was freezing cold and yet burning up, all at once.

You'll wake up tomorrow, I told myself. You'll wake up tomorrow morning and this will all have been a dream.

It had to be.

I was drying my face on some kitchen towel when the doorbell rang. Mrs Tout . . . or Andrew.

I went to open the door. Immediately, Andrew stepped into the house. He grinned at me.

'That's better,' he said. 'Come here.'

He was OK again. His eyes were bright, his whole body relaxed.

'Please,' he cajoled. He held out his hands. Slowly, almost reluctantly I took them in mine. They weren't cold any more.

'W-why are your hands so hot all of a sudden?'

A terrible thought crept into my head and refused to go away. He looked at me without saying a word, his cheeks flushed, his lips red. I clamped my teeth together.

'What do you want me to say? I hadn't fed since yesterday. I was hungry, feeling faint.'

'And your food?' I whispered.

'There was a cat . . . in a garden a few doors down . . .'

I turned my head. I was going to be sick. Just a hair's breadth away from throwing up.

'Don't look like that.' Andrew's voice was bitter. 'A car needs petrol to run. You need food. It just happens that I need blood. I have to, Heather. I'll die otherwise.'

I didn't trust myself to speak until my stomach quietened. I kept swallowing hard.

'Besides, I put the cat in the dustbin when I'd finished.'

'That's hardly the point,' I said furiously. 'This isn't about whether or not you tidy up after you've finished. It's about what you do. It's about what you are. You're a . . . a . . .'

'Say it.'

I breathed deeply, trying to catch my breath.

'Say it.' He grasped my upper arms. His hands were like vices.

'Andrew, you're hurting me,' I gasped, pushing at his chest. He released me at once.

'I'm sorry, Heather,' he said quietly. 'I didn't mean to. I forgot I'm a lot stronger when I've just . . . I'm sorry.'

I rubbed my upper arms. They were sore as hell. I'd have painful bruises there by morning.

'Heather, I need to know . . . how you feel about me . . . about us.'

Andrew watched me. He didn't blink once. He looked as if he could read all the thoughts in my head, almost before I became aware of them.

'I love you. You know that,' I whispered.

'But?'

'No buts.'

Silence.

'Heather, what are you going to do?' he asked quietly.

'About what?'

'About us? About the way . . . about the way I am now?'

'I don't see that there is much I can do about it,' I said unhappily.

'I see.'

'No, you don't see,' I shook my head. 'I'm frightened, Andrew. Is it really true? Are you really . . .' I couldn't finish.

'Yes.' Andrew's answer was immediate.

'Can't you do something . . . ? Is there no way to change you back?'

'I don't want to be changed back.' His voice was hard. 'I'm strong, powerful. I can do things now that I'd never even dreamt of before.'

There was something in his voice, some new note that I'd never heard before.

'But earlier you said . . . you said that you were scared,' I reminded him.

'Only of one thing.'

'Which is?' I whispered, afraid I already knew the answer.

There was a long pause before Andrew answered. 'That you won't join me.'

'But Andrew, you're . . . you're . . .'

'You still can't say it, can you?' he mocked.

I didn't reply. How could I say it? It was such a ridiculous word. It conjured up images of gothic castles and wild horsemen and red contact lenses and yet, here before me, was Andrew. Not like the film images at all. *Almost* normal.

'I'm still the same person, Heather. You can see that, can't you?'

'I guess . . . How does it make you feel, inside?'

'I told you. Powerful. In control.'

'No, I'm not talking about physically. I'm talking about . . . emotionally.'

93

'That depends.'

'On what?'

'On whether or not you join me.' He looked at me.

'So we're back to that?'

'Let me make you the same as me. Let me drink from you.'

I swallowed hard. This was it. Yes or no. A new, strange existence with Andrew, or a life without him.

The choice was mine.

Fifteen

'Andrew, it's not that simple. I need time to think.'

'About what?'

'Stop it,' I cried out. 'Stop rushing me. Stop using how I feel about you against me.'

'I'm not . . .'

'Yes, you are. I still can't believe that you're . . . I didn't even think they really existed. Now you're standing there saying not only are you a . . . a . . . but you want to make me one too. The thought of it turns my stomach. It's disgusting . . .' I broke off abruptly when I realised what I'd said. Andrew looked like I'd slapped him. 'Andrew, I didn't mean . . .'

'Yes you did.'

Silence.

'Please. Just give me until tomorrow. That's all I'm asking. I have to think.'

'All right then. Have it your own way. I'll come round tomorrow evening.'

I nodded gratefully. 'So where are you going now? Home?'

'I guess so. I've nowhere else to go,' he said.

It took all of my resolve not to ask him to stay with me. God knows I wanted to. I think that even though we were together, neither of us had ever felt so lonely.

'I think you should go home before your mum has me arrested for abducting you,' I said at last.

'I'll see you tomorrow.'

I watched him leave the house and walk down the street. He turned back to me for a few moments, saying nothing, before he continued on his way. I shut the front door. Tomorrow. I'd wait 'til tomorrow. Maybe there was a way out of this for Andrew, and me. Maybe he was only saying he didn't want to change because he thought he *couldn't* change.

But first things first. Right now, all I wanted to do was fall into bed and sleep. And maybe I would sleep my troubles away. Mum always said that things look better in the morning.

Monday afternoon was beautiful. I woke up with sunlight streaming through my window and warming my face. I felt better, not good but better. I had a long, cool shower and trotted downstairs for a late, late breakfast. Only once I was in the kitchen, I wasn't hungry any more. I rattled around like a lone pea in a tin can. I opened the fridge and closed it. Opened cupboard doors and closed them. I sighed, about to give up when the doorbell rang unexpectedly, making me jump.

Andrew? God, I hadn't expected him to come around so early. The bell rang again. Wiping my sweaty hands on some kitchen towel, I went to open the door. It was Pete.

'Hello, Pete. Come in.' I smiled, stepping aside for him.

'Hiya, Heather. You're pleased to see me,' he said surprised. Then his eyes narrowed. 'What are you after? I don't owe you money, do I?'

'Of course not!' I said, shutting the door behind him.

We went into the kitchen. I poured myself a glass of orange juice and sat down.

'D'you mind if I have one?' Pete asked.

'Sorry, Pete! Help yourself. I've got a lot on my mind.'

'Yeah, I can guess.' He frowned. 'He hasn't turned up yet then?'

I didn't answer.

'I just popped round to see how you were after last night. Is there anything I can do for you?' he asked, his head buried in the fridge.

I shrugged as I watched him. 'No, but thanks for offering.'

Pete looked round and smiled at me. If he and I had been an item, my life would be so uncomplicated, in more ways than one.

'What are you thinking? You look wistful.'

'I was just wondering what it would have been like to go out with you – if you hadn't stood me up on our first date. Do you remember?'

'Yes, I remember,' he said quietly. His smile disappeared.

'Why *did* you stand me up?'

'I wanted to explain at the time, but you weren't in the mood to listen and Andrew was always nearby.'

'What's Andrew got to do with it?'

Pete straightened up, a carton of milk in his hand. Frown lines creased his forehead. 'Heather, are you and Andrew still going strong?'

'Yes. I guess . . .' I replied. 'You'd better sniff that before you drink any.'

Pete swirled the milk around in its carton. He opened his mouth only to close it again without speaking.

'Look, I'm not telling you this to stir up trouble between you and Andrew. But I do want to clear the air on this one.'

'What are you talking about?' I asked, my orange juice forgotten in my hands.

'I didn't stand you up, Heather. Or rather I didn't meet you outside the cinema like we'd planned, but I did send you a message to say I couldn't make it.'

'I didn't get any message.'

'I know.' His face was grim.

'Did you leave a message with my mum?' I voiced

my suspicion. Mum was really bad at passing on my messages.

He shook his head. I was getting impatient.

'Stop being so mysterious, Pete Shorman. What happened?'

'I . . . I asked someone to tell you that I wouldn't be able to make it,' he said quietly.

'Who?'

'Can't you guess?'

'Pete, for heaven's sake . . .' I stared at him. 'You don't mean . . .'

'I asked Andrew to tell you,' he said quietly.

'You can't be serious. *My* Andrew?' I stared at him.

'Maybe I shouldn't have said anything . . .'

Why do people say what they want only to wonder if they shouldn't have said it at all afterwards?!

'Let me get this straight. You asked Andrew to tell me you couldn't make it to our first date and instead of passing on your message, he took me out instead?'

Pete shrugged. 'That's about right.'

'I don't believe it. Andrew would never do anything so . . . so underhand,' I protested vehemently.

I stared at him. I couldn't believe it. I *wouldn't* believe it. Andrew wouldn't do something like that, I knew he wouldn't.

Pete looked at me, then burst out laughing. 'You have to admit, Heather, I did get you going for a while.'

'Pete, you swine! I should brain you. I thought you were serious,' I said, shaking my head.

'I'm good, aren't I?'

'Very,' I agreed ruefully. 'So are you going to tell me why you stood me up or not?'

'Where do you keep your glasses?' he asked.

Impatiently, I pointed to the low-level cupboard opposite the cooker. He took out a glass and poured himself some milk, slowly swirling it around before drinking it.

'Well?' I asked.

'It's as you thought. I simply forgot we had a date.'

I should've been annoyed, insulted at the very least, but I wasn't.

'At least you're honest,' I said dryly.

'Aren't I just,' he said, before knocking back his milk. 'Come on then. If you've finished stuffing your face, let's go out somewhere. It'll stop you worrying about Andrew for a while.'

'Is it that obvious?'

'Heather, you have a face like an illustrated book.' Pete smiled.

I thought about it. Should I wait for Andrew? But how could I? I didn't know what time he'd turn up. I thought about phoning him but decided against it. I was missing him, but what we both needed were a few hours away from each other. Time to think. I still hadn't worked out what we were going to do, what *I* was going to do.

But I had to make up my mind, and soon.

Sixteen

We spent the rest of the day together. We just ambled about, talking. Pete didn't even mind when I suggested that we go into town to do some window shopping. Andrew hated that sort of thing. The hours flew by until finally we hopped on a bus and came back home. We bought a take-away pizza and started walking back to my house. It was a beautiful evening. Scattered cotton-wool clouds blotted the sky, and the low sun was so orange it was burning a hole in the sky's deep blue. I raised my face, my eyes closed, enjoying the feel of the fading sunlight on my face. It was delicious.

'I never figured you for a sun worshipper.' Pete smiled.

'Who wouldn't be on a day like today?'

'It *has* been fun,' he agreed.

Once home, we sat in the living-room eating the pizza. Pete was good company. He seemed to know when to speak, and when to stay silent. Just the occasional smile as we sat eating our pizzas was enough. With a start I realised what it was about him that comforted me. He was normal. He represented normality when everything else around me was topsy-turvy. To think that I should find something so ordinary so attractive.

The living-room was getting darker. I stood up and went to the window to close the curtains. As I looked out of the window I could see that the sun had set.

'What're you doing?' Pete asked, moving to stand behind me.

100

'Watching the sky before it gets dark.'

'Come and watch me thrash you at *Tomb Raider* instead.'

I wasn't really in the mood for a video game – how could I be when the only thing I had on my mind was Andrew? – but I smiled and closed the curtains, wondering why Andrew hadn't even phoned me yet. Would he come to see me like he said he would? Or would he give up and not bother? The Andrew I knew would never give up. He'd have been here hours ago.

Pete switched on the telly and set up the game. He started first and within five minutes he'd been zapped.

'That was so tired!' I scoffed. 'I could do better than that with just one finger on the controller.'

'Go on then if you're so bad,' Pete challenged.

I picked up my controller. It took me less than two minutes to get further than Pete. Then to my annoyance the doorbell rang.

'Oh Pete, could you get that?' I said. 'It's probably Mrs Tout. Don't let the nosy old bat in, whatever you do.'

Pete stood up and went to answer the bell. The next thing I heard was the front door being slammed shut violently and a commotion in the hall. Leaping to my feet, I ran in to the hall. Then I saw something that chilled my soul.

Andrew, his face puce with rage, held Pete up in the air above his head. Pete was shouting to be put down. His eyes were furious, and terrified. He couldn't believe what was happening. Andrew stepped forward, his arms tensing.

'NO...ANDREW!' I screamed. 'Please no. *Don't.*' I rushed forward to where Andrew would have thrown Pete. 'Andrew, put him down. Please! *Please!*'

'What's he doing here?' Andrew asked furiously.

'Eating pizza and playing video games. That's all,' I said quickly. 'Put him down.'

Andrew glared at me. I stared at him. This Andrew I'd never seen before. His face was hard and gaunt and his eyes were like lasers burning straight into me. Then he took a deep breath and his body relaxed. He closed his eyes briefly and when he opened them again my Andrew was back. Slowly he lowered his arms and set Pete down.

'What the hell do you think you're doing?' yelled Pete.

Andrew was still looking at me as Pete drew back his arm and, making a fist, swung for him. He caught the punch so quickly that I didn't even see his hand move. And he was still looking at me.

'Go away, Pete. I want to talk to Heather,' he said quietly.

'I'm not leaving her with you,' Pete said furiously, pulling away his hand.

'Yes you are.' For the first time Andrew turned to look at Pete, and Pete flinched, his head moving back slightly.

'Go on, Pete. I'll be okay. I'll see you tomorrow.' I didn't want him in a fight he couldn't win.

'Heather, are you really going to be all right?' Pete said after a long pause.

'Of course I am.' I tried to smile and failed miserably. 'Thanks for coming to see me today.'

'Are you sure you want me to leave?'

I nodded.

'I'm coming round to see you first thing tomorrow morning,' he said, glaring at Andrew.

'No, it's okay. I'll phone you – I promise.'

Two spots of colour, red as blood, appeared on Andrew's cheeks. I went to walk around Andrew to see Pete to the door but Andrew caught my arm and wouldn't let me past, so I watched as Pete stepped out of the house. He cast one last look at me.

'I'll see you tomorrow,' he said.

I smiled unhappily. He shut the door. I stretched out my fingers.

'Take your damned hand of me,' I hissed up at Andrew, pulling away from him. 'Who the hell do you think you are? Morgan?'

It was as if a dam had burst inside me and I couldn't control the rage spewing out of my mouth.

'You shouldn't have let him in here . . .' Andrew began.

'Oh! And just when did my mum sell this house to you? If I want the whole of the Liverpool football team in here, there's not a damn thing you can do or say about it. Just what did you think you were doing, lifting Pete up like that?'

He turned to face me but said nothing.

'How dare you humiliate me like that? What's the matter with you? Did that man in Fipoli suck out your brains as well as your blood?'

Still he said nothing. Somehow that made what had happened worse. I wanted to lash out and hurt him. I burned to hurt him. So I slapped him. He didn't flinch. He didn't even blink.

'You pig! I'm sorry I ever laid eyes on you,' I shouted. 'You disgust me. And you want to turn me into the same as you? Well, I won't do it. I won't. I won't. You turn my stomach.'

I saw him swallow. Just that. He swallowed and I knew I'd gone too far.

Seventeen

Andrew turned away from me. His hunched shoulders made him seem like an old man. He walked towards the front door and opened it.

'I-I'm sorry, Heather,' he said quietly, his back to me, 'I won't trouble you again.'

He went out of the house, closing the door slowly behind him.

'Andrew . . .'

He didn't close the door but he didn't open it either. I waited. He waited.

'Andrew, don't . . . don't go.'

An eternity passed. Slowly Andrew walked back into the house, his head bent. He shut the door carefully behind him before leaning his forehead against it, his back to me. I couldn't see his face, his expression. What was he thinking? Was he as unhappy as I was?

So this was it. The moment of decision. It was up to me now. We were a sigh's breadth away from splitting up. And I didn't want that to happen. God knows I didn't.

'M-make me the same as you.' It was a struggle to get the words out. 'M-make it so that we can be together . . .'

'Why?'

He still hadn't turned around. It made what I had to say easier.

'Because I'm miserable. Because we're not the same any more. But because I'd rather be miserable with you than without you.'

'Once you're the same as me, there'll be no going back.'

'I know.'

He straightened up and turned around to face me.

'I'm sorry about Pete. I lost my temper.'

'You had no reason to.'

'I know. I see that now.'

He stood at the front door. I stood by the stairs. Why were we so far apart? I was confused. I did love him, but what he was, what he *did*, still turned me off.

Looking at Andrew now, I tried to tell myself that he was still the same. *We* were still the same. We loved each other. We had the rest of our lives together. So why couldn't I get over this feeling that what I was about to do was very, very wrong? What was that ancient Beatles song called? *All You Need Is Love*? Well, I was about to find out whether or not that was true.

'So what happens next?'

'When are your mum and Jessica coming home?'

'Not until Saturday.'

'Then let's go upstairs.'

At his words, I shook physically. I was more than nervous, I was scared. And ashamed because I felt scared.

Once in my room, he sat in my chair whilst I sat on the very edge of the bed. My stomach knotted with tension. Strangely, I wanted to laugh. Laugh and laugh and never stop. All day I'd avoided even thinking about this moment. As if by not thinking about it, I could stop it from happening. Now here I was, caught up in something I couldn't understand or control.

'What happens now? Do you take blood from my wrist or what?'

Andrew shrugged. 'Your wrist, your neck. Where doesn't matter.'

'Will it hurt?'

He nodded slowly. If he'd said or done otherwise, I wouldn't have believed him. 'Then you'll be out of it for a while but, when you wake up, you'll be . . .'

'Like you,' I finished. 'Let's get on with it.'

There are no such things as blood drinkers . . . No such things . . . no such things . . .

Except for the man in Fipoli and the man in my room and in just a little while . . .

'Are you sure?' Andrew said.

I swallowed hard. 'Yes. Don't worry. I'm not going to change my mind.'

'All right, then.'

'All right, then. Do you know exactly what you have to do?'

There was a discernible pause before he nodded. 'Don't worry. I won't let anything happen to you.'

'Well, the sooner we start, the sooner it'll be over.' Get it over, I thought. I just want it to be over.

Andrew stood up and came over to sit next to me. 'Are you afraid?'

'Petrified!' I looked directly at him. I wasn't joking.

'Don't be. In a little while you'll be immortal.'

His eyes were turning ice cold again. I could hear my heart pounding, pounding, pounding in my chest.

Don't do it . . . do it . . . don't do it . . .

The words played over and over in my head.

'Are you going to drink my blood?' I whispered.

'Yes. I . . . Yes.'

I lowered my gaze, then turned away, trying to frame my next question. There had to be another way. We could be together without this . . . couldn't we? He folded his arms around my neck to hug me close to him. I leaned back. He felt warm, safe. Still my Andrew. I shuffled up to get as close to him as possible. Suddenly, he leapt back, as if stung.

106

'What's the matter?' I turned around, surprised.

He looked from my face to my throat and back again. He smiled.

'Your cross,' he gestured. 'It dug into me. Could you take it off?'

'But I always wear it. Why do I have to . . . ?'

'Come on, Heather. Please take it off.'

Frowning, I turned my back to him. 'Undo it for me then?'

'No can do. Sorry,' he said lightly. He wriggled his fingers before me. 'I'm all thumbs. I wouldn't be able to manage the clasp.'

Puzzled by his refusal, I unclasped the necklace myself. Then a strange, horrific idea entered my head. So horrific I almost laughed out loud. It was preposterous. I held my silver cross on its silver necklace out to Andrew. He immediately drew back. Suddenly it wasn't so funny any more.

'That's not clever, Heather. You startled me.' He sat forward to resume his former position, his eyes never leaving the cross in my hand. Slowly, I coiled my fingers around it. It felt warm and comforting. I squeezed it until it dug into my palm, hurting.

Carefully, I placed my necklace in the top drawer of my bedside table. I stared down at the now closed drawer, afraid, sad. Andrew placed a hand under my chin, turning me round to face him. He was still smiling. I wished he wouldn't.

'Promise me something?'

'Anything.'

'Promise me that if . . . if I do this . . . you won't leave me until I wake up. Promise me you won't leave me alone in this house.'

'There's something I have to do. It shouldn't take too long . . .'

'It'll have to wait. Can't it wait? Promise me.'

'I promise. I won't go any further than your garden.'

He smiled. Now he looked the same as before we went on holiday – before any of this had happened. Almost. Looking at him I tried to believe that what I was about to do was something strange and weird and wonderful. So many other people would give up everything for a chance like this. Yet here I was, with the chance right in front of me. All I had to do was reach out and take it. And still I hesitated. This was something to ensure that Andrew and I were together forever. Forever . . .

Isn't that what I wanted?

He kissed the side of my neck, sending a shiver racing through my body. I held on tightly to his warm, warm hands. He kissed my neck again.

'You're salty.'

I could hear the smile in his voice.

My blood roared in my ears like a storm-swept sea. Forever . . . as a . . . blood drinker.

I couldn't.

Lies. It was all lies. He shouldn't be kissing me. Not when what we were about to do was so . . . *so wrong*. What would I be? What would I become? Time. I needed more time.

Do it . . . don't do it . . . do it . . .

'No . . . NO!' I screamed, and pulled away violently. I leapt to my feet. I fought to catch my breath. *Why couldn't I breathe?*

'I'm s-sorry . . . I can't . . .' I ran to the door.

He was there before me, facing me, his back against the door. Stunned, I stared at him. A moment ago he'd been sitting on my bed.

'How . . . ?' I shut up. Then I tried again. 'Andrew, I can't do this. Please understand. You're going too fast. I'm frightened.'

'Trust me.' He smiled, but his eyes . . . his eyes didn't

smile. They didn't blink, they stared at me. Only it was more than just staring. His eyes lasered me.

'Trust me.' His voice was so gentle, so soft. He reached out his hand towards me, slowly. Oh, so slowly.

'Trust me.'

Why did he keep saying that? Over and over? And staring?

Don't . . .

My hand was in his and my body was next to his as he hugged me, and I had no idea how I'd got there. I wasn't even aware that I'd moved from the middle of the room.

'Andrew . . .' I had to fight to get the words out. 'P-please . . . more time . . . one more day . . . *Please . . .*'

'Heather, trust me.' His voice was no more than a sigh. A breath of the faintest, warmest air caressed my ear, my throat. My eyes were closing. I fought against it.

Do it . . . don't do it . . .

Andrew . . . don't . . . Were the words only in my head or did I speak them?

It's wrong . . . it's right . . . wrong . . . don't . . .

I don't want this . . . It's wrong . . .

'Trust me . . .'

And he bit me.

Eighteen

It hurt. It hurt like hell. Instantly it felt as if my neck was on fire. And that fire spread over my face and down my body. Along with the frantic hammering of my heart, I could hear him gulping. My blood. The sound made my stomach churn, it was disgusting. And the burning in my neck was getting hotter. At that moment I tried to pull away but his hands were like vices holding mine.

Don't do it . . .

This was a huge mistake. I loved Andrew but this wasn't right. I tried to speak but my tongue felt about fifty times its normal size and so dry. I tried to take a stronger hold of his hands in mine but I didn't seem to be able to move. Mum and Jessica and Pete and Diane . . . everyone I knew seemed to drift into my head to stand before me. My eyelids fluttered open. The pounding of my heart was subsiding. I could hardly hear it now. I was so tired, so sleepy. It didn't hurt so much any more. But I could still hear him drinking. My blood. Slurping, gulping sounds. But now they too were far away. Outside of me.

My head was so heavy. My eyes closed, I let my head nod forward. I'd never felt so weary. Bone and blood weary. Then I was being carried, then gently lowered on to the bed. It was a struggle to open my eyes again. I only just managed it. Just in time to see his flushed red face smiling down at me. A tiny trickle of blood escaped from the corner of his mouth and began to dribble down towards his chin. His tongue snaked out after it and licked it up.

Not me . . . not a drinker . . . not me . . .

His lips were the reddest I had ever seen them. I fought to keep my eyes open.

Something was wrong.

I was slipping away from my body. That's the only way I can describe it. It wasn't like daydreaming or even sleeping, it was deeper than that. I couldn't feel any part of my body, I couldn't even feel my heartbeat now. All I was aware of was a faint throbbing in my neck. I was slipping away. I tried to speak, to say Andrew's name but I couldn't.

Then I realised I was dying.

'Don't worry, Heather. I'm here.' Andrew's voice reached me through acres of cotton wool. 'Don't close your eyes. Not yet.'

Past the fluttering of my eyelids I saw him bite deeply into his own wrist. Immediately he put it over my mouth.

You must be joking, I thought with disgust. The thought had me fighting back to consciousness. It was the strongest thought I'd had since he'd bitten me.

Not me . . .

I turned my head away, but not far enough.

'You must,' he said urgently. 'You can't survive if you don't.'

He turned my head and placed his wrist against my lips. I gagged as the hot, rust-flavoured liquid ran down my throat, but I couldn't move away. My stomach started to burn.

'Drink, Heather,' he ordered.

If I'd had the choice, if I could have told him, I would have chosen to die rather than drink his blood. As Andrew's blood continued to fill my mouth I wanted to curl up and hide where no one could find me.

I tried not to swallow, I tried to cough out the sour liquid, but he pinched my nostrils together so I had to gulp to clear my mouth . . . so I could breathe. And still Andrew held his wrist over my mouth.

'This is how Julius kept me alive in Fipoli,' his voice was far, far away. I could only just hear it. 'I would've died otherwise . . . Heather . . .'

I didn't hear any more. I forced myself not to hear any more.

My eyelids were made of lead. I couldn't have opened my eyes now, even if I'd wanted to, and I didn't want to. I didn't want to see anything, least of all Andrew's face. My stomach was cramped up. I felt foul. I was foul. I was disgusting. I wanted to cry, to howl.

Once again he held my hands in his, saying something, and although I could hear the sounds I couldn't make out the words. The sounds grew more distant. My body grew more and more heavy until I thought I must surely sink through the mattress. I pushed at Andrew's hands, at least I think I did.

Then I gave in and allowed myself to pass out.

Nineteen

Waking up was like rushing upwards through fathoms of water to surface and gasp for air. I awoke icy cold, but bathed in sweat. A whole dance troupe was doing the running man in my head.

And I was hungry.

Ravenously, gnawingly, achingly hungry. My stomach felt as if it was about to collapse in on itself. I struggled to sit up. I looked around the darkened room. Something was different. With a start of half fear, half excitement I realised what it was. I could see – perfectly.

The curtains were drawn and I instinctively knew it was late at night – but I could see perfectly. I could see colours. They didn't look the same as when viewed by daylight but they were colours nonetheless. Night colours, muted but somehow with a life of their own. Each colour in my room seemed to hum out at me, the grotty pink of the wallpaper behind my posters, my pale yellow bottle of baby lotion on the dressing table. Was this new? Or had I just never noticed it before? I continued to scan the room. I could read Van Gogh's signature on my poster of his sunflowers. I could even read the words on the bottle of baby lotion, and I could see . . .

'Andrew . . . ?'

He was sitting on my bedroom chair next to the dressing table, watching me.

'Hello, Heather.' His voice was strange, sort of hard

and happy. Uncertainly, I watched him. He smiled back at me, his eyes dark and glinting.

'You bit me.' Was it a statement or a question? I wasn't sure. I wasn't sure of anything any more. The line between what was real and what was unreal had faded into non-existence. He didn't reply. I searched for something innocuous to say. 'How long have I been asleep?'

'One day and a night. This is your second night.'

'A whole day! I can't have been out for a whole day.' He nodded.

'It didn't take you that long to wake up,' I said, confused.

'D'you remember the drinks Julius gave us in Fipoli?'

'Yeah, some sort of wine cocktail.'

'It wasn't wine. Well, not all wine. His blood was mixed in as well, that and a mild sedative. It meant that I was over the effects of the change a lot faster than you. I had his blood in my system to begin with. You didn't.'

'You *did* bite me then?'

He didn't move, he didn't blink. He just kept watching me. I could see him clearly, as if the sun were just outside my bedroom window. I stretched out my hand towards the lamp on my bedside table. All at once I felt more than nervous, almost afraid. Seeing so well in the dark wasn't natural. It wasn't *ordinary*. At that moment I needed the ordinary. Lamplight was ordinary. The sudden light didn't even make me blink.

'What did you do to me?' My memory was limping back now. 'You stopped me from leaving... My God... You stopped me...'

'No, I didn't. I asked you to trust me. And you did.' He shrugged and smiled.

That memory filled my head now. Maybe I'd got the

114

rest wrong. If only my head would clear, but I felt so peculiar. I forced myself to concentrate.

My name is Heather Lucas and I'm seventeen years old. At least my brain still worked.

And I felt the same as before, except for my stomach. I was a little light-headed, perhaps, and weak, but just the same?

'It worked, didn't it?' I whispered.

He nodded, the smile still on his face. It was as if every part of my body were waiting, but I didn't know for what.

'I can see through the dark . . . Is that part of it?'

He nodded again.

'Apart from that, I don't feel much different.'

'You will.'

Was it a threat or a promise? Then more of what happened came back to me. Without warning, Andrew sprang out of his chair and came over to me. He sat down on the bed taking my ice-cold hands in his. The memory limp turned into a sprint.

'You . . . you made me drink . . .'

I closed my eyes and again saw Andrew biting into his wrist and holding it over my mouth. I remembered the churning disgust I'd felt as his blood flowed over my tongue. Deep within me, a knot of dread began to unravel. I started to tremble. I pulled my hands out of his and wrapped them around my waist. The trembling was getting worse – deep inside me but spreading out-wards like ripples in a pond.

'You *made* me drink . . .' I whispered again. I stretched out my fingers until my bones cracked. It was that or lash out and scream and never stop. Even now my stomach turned over at the memory.

'I had to. It wouldn't have worked otherwise. I wasn't even sure how much to drink from you. I had to try

115

and remember all I could of what happened to me and gauge it that way.'

'You . . . you never told me that.'

'You wouldn't have let me do it otherwise. Besides, I wouldn't have let anything happen to you. No way.'

I shut my eyes tight. Every detail of what had happened filled my head. I covered my ears with my hands. My head was about to split open.

'You wanted to be like me. You wanted us to be together.'

'Not like this.'

'Exactly like this. You could have stopped me at any time.'

'You're a liar. How could I?' I couldn't stop shaking.

'Heather, I love you. I want us to be together. If you were me, wouldn't you have done the same thing?'

I froze, staring at him, wondering if it were true. I spread out my fingers and stretched and stretched them.

'Besides, it's wonderful! Can't you feel how powerful you are? We've both been reborn as something beyond our wildest dreams. Can't you feel it?' Andrew breathed deeply, delight on his face.

A flare of anger shot up in me at his attitude, but it faded just as quickly. Andrew loved me. I loved him. We could be together now. We were the same. And that was all that mattered, *wasn't it* . . . ?

'I thought from all those Hammer Horror films that all you had to do was . . . bite me?'

He grinned. 'It's not that simple. It takes the blood of a vampire to make a vampire.'

I shuddered. 'I still can't get used to that word.'

'The word doesn't matter. You can call yourself what you like. It's what you are that counts. And isn't it *terrific*? Isn't it exciting? It was worth it, wasn't it? You're one of us now . . .'

'Us? Who are you talking about?'

'Us. Julius and me and all the others out there like us. There are bound to be more.'

'Julius made more?'

'Only two more.' Andrew grinned. 'At least that's what he told me. He told me what to expect. How to survive. He thought he owed me that much. He liked you, you know. He liked both of us. That's why he didn't kill us, even though he could have. Instead he brought me back to life.'

Kill us . . . ? No . . . *Don't think* . . . Julius was someone else's problem . . .

'Back to life? You said something about that when you . . . when you gave me your blood.' I lowered my head.

'So you *do* remember.'

'Some of it. Not all of it.' The shaking was over, except for my stomach. I shivered. I was beginning to feel cold and a little dizzy.

'I don't feel too well.'

'I've got a surprise for you.' He smiled at me. 'It's something that will make you feel a whole lot better. Follow me.'

'I hope it's a hot bath.'

'It's something much better.'

I got out of bed and followed him downstairs, through the kitchen, in to the back garden. The only light came from the moon which kept disappearing behind silver clouds. The air smelt fresh and warm, the wind stroked at my face. I breathed deeply, which only made me feel worse. I could hear strange sounds, like being in an electrical shop and hearing the noise of twenty televisions on different channels all at once. I could hear what sounded like Mr Travis from four doors down, arguing with his wife about the cost of their dinner. I heard canned laughter from someone's telly, and I heard what I was sure was Mrs Tout crying.

117

I shook my head, trying to shake all the sounds out of it.

'You'll get used to that.' Andrew smiled at me. 'Just tune out. Don't concentrate on any sounds that you don't want. The rest will soon fade.'

I tried to concentrate on not concentrating. To my surprise it worked, sort of. I could still hear noises but the sensation was like a distant buzzing rather than something inside my head.

'Where on earth are we going?'

Anxiously, I glanced up at Mrs Tout's back windows. Was she up there, watching us? I wondered why she was crying. I was sure I was right about that. I tried to concentrate on hearing just her, but the sounds from all the other houses came back as well. I tuned out. The buzzing came back. Something for me to practise. But I was still normal . . .

He took my hand and led me towards the bottom of the garden. The dry grass crunched under my feet. I didn't dare glance down. I dreaded to think what I was stepping on. All those creepy crawlies that only emerged at night. Ugh!

All at once, the garden began to rock and sway. I put my hand to my temple. My stomach pains were getting worse.

'Andrew, something's wrong. My head's spinning. And I'm hungry. And I feel sick.'

'I know. That's now I felt in Julius' house when I woke up.'

'Will it pass?'

'Soon. Very soon.'

We'd reached the bottom of the garden now. The branches of our neighbour's horse-chestnut tree hung down over one half of our back fence.

'Stay here.'

Then, as I watched, Andrew vaulted over the back

fence into our opposite neighbour's garden. He put his hands on what was an almost two metres-high fence and leapt over it as if it were no more than a twig on the ground. I stared after him, unable to believe my eyes.

But why was I so surprised? Hadn't Andrew lifted up Pete as though he were a pillow? Andrew was super strong and super fast and he could hear a pin drop two streets away.

Was I the same? *Could* I be the same? Did it just take practice, or was there more to it than that?

I felt so strange. I put my hand to my forehead. Something was wrong. My mind was reeling madly now, my body freezing. I was about to collapse.

'Here we are!' Andrew appeared from nowhere to stand before me. In his hands he held Juniper, the grey and white rabbit which belonged to Mr and Mrs Rossotti's son, Matthew.

'What've you got Juniper for? You'd better put him back before Matthew misses him.'

I shook my head again to clear it. My words seemed to be uncertain and slurred. The moonlight vanished as the moon disappeared behind a dark cloud. The only dim light came from the back windows of the surrounding houses. By rights I shouldn't have been able to see a thing. Yet I could see clearly.

'Andrew . . . ?'

'You have to feed, Heather,' he said softly. 'If you don't drink, you'll die.'

I looked from Andrew to Juniper, and back again. 'You must be joking. I'm not . . . put him back.'

Slowly Andrew shook his head. 'You must drink, Heather.'

'Never!'

I turned to make for the house. My legs gave way under me. I fell to my knees. I struggled to stand up again but I couldn't. My head was reeling. Andrew knelt down before me, Juniper still in his hands. Then he held Juniper out to me in both his hands and . . . and . . .

He killed it. At the smell of blood, my mouth filled with saliva. I ran my tongue over my teeth. My top canine teeth were longer than a few seconds ago – and razor sharp. I gasped. Andrew had warned me that it would happen, but it was still a shock.

He made me drink – when I was too weak to push his hands away. No, I take that back. He made me take my first sip. And the first sip stopped my head from reeling and took away the dizzy feeling and made the cramps in my stomach disappear and tasted . . .

And tasted . . . So I drank.

To my shame and my horror and my disgust . . . *I drank*.

Twenty

When I'd finished, I looked down at the ground. Andrew's warm hands cupped my face, so I had to look at him. He looked happy. I wished it was contagious.

'How are you feeling now? Less dizzy? Stronger?'

'Yeah, I'm okay now. What about you?'

'I drank earlier. I didn't want to miss a moment with you when you woke up.'

We walked back into the house. I asked something that was bothering me, choking me.

'How often must we . . . ?'

'Every day.'

'Isn't there some other way?'

He shook his head, and moved to stand in front of me. 'You can eat and drink what you like, but it won't make any difference. Only blood makes a difference.'

'What did you . . . feed on w-when I was . . . unconscious?'

'Anything I could from your garden. I promised I wouldn't leave you and I didn't. I didn't leave, Heather.'

'I h-hate this. I can't do this.'

'Shush!' Andrew kissed me. 'You'll get used to it. It'll be like breathing, like eating every day to survive. Just something you have to do.'

'But it shouldn't be like that. It shouldn't be something you get used to.'

'We've got no choice.'

There was nothing I could say to that.

We were both silent for many minutes. I lowered my

head. Sadness, quiet and still, wrapped around me like a velvet cloak.

'What day is it?'

'Tuesday. Why?'

'Mum and Jessica are coming home on Saturday. That's something at least.' I sighed. 'I miss them. I think I'll go to the airport on Saturday morning to meet them.'

'You can't.'

'Pardon?'

'You'll have to wait until Saturday night to see them. You and I must sleep during the day. Sunlight will kill us.' I stared at him until my eyes hurt.

'You mean we have to sleep in a coffin filled with earth and . . . ?'

'Slow down. Of course not. We just have to sleep somewhere where daylight can't get to us. Then we wake up when the sun goes down.'

'I'll never see the sun again? You don't mean it.'

Andrew shrugged. 'I'm sorry. I thought you'd realised.'

'Sorry!' I closed my eyes. 'I'll never see the sun again . . .'

'We have other things that ordinary people don't have to make up for it.'

Other things . . . but not daylight and sunshine. I couldn't take it in. What would life be like without daylight? I clasped my hands together tightly in my lap.

'Where were you sleeping . . . before all this? At your house? How have you made sure that daylight doesn't get to you?'

'I've been sleeping in the attic, temporarily. I thought you and I could stay here in your room until your mum and sister get back, and in the meantime we can start looking for something more permanent.'

'You mean you want us to live together?' I asked, surprised.

'It would make sense. We could protect each other that way. And we'd be together all the time. I'd love that. Wouldn't you?'

A month ago, when it would have been just an impossible, out-of-reach fantasy, then yes. But now . . .?

'I guess . . . If we don't find somewhere permanent before Mum and Jessica get home, where will we stay? In your attic?'

Andrew nodded.

'Is it safe?'

'Yeah, just as long as a pipe doesn't burst, and that's not likely in autumn. That's the only reason my dad ever goes up there.'

'What about Morgan? And your mum?'

'Mum in the attic! Do me a favour! And why would Morgan go up there?'

'We could stay there, then, for a while until we found somewhere really safe. If we were careful.' I considered the proposition. It didn't appeal.

'How do we get up there past your family?'

'We have to jump up on to the conservatory roof, up on to the part of the roof over the back bedroom and then walk up the slates to the sky-light,' Andrew said, as if he was giving instructions for getting to the end of the road.

'Just how do we jump more than ten feet? Turn into bats?'

'Don't be sarky. We bend our knees and jump. You'd be surprised at what we can do once we've fed. I've done it already.'

'Have you?' I was surprised.

'Of course, with plenty of room to spare. And as you're always telling me, anything a mere man can do a woman can do better!' Andrew smiled. I couldn't smile back.

Silence.

123

'Andrew, I'm scared.'

'We'll be all right. We've got each other now.'

I nodded, slowly. 'What was it like when it was . . . just you?'

'Let's just say I wouldn't want to go through that again.' His smile faded. 'It was the worst time of my life.'

'And that's why you wanted me to join you? For company?'

'That reason was way down on my list,' Andrew replied with a frown. 'Heather, I wanted you with me. To share all this power. We're strong, invincible. Can't you feel it?'

'Invincible? Daylight will kill us. Not drinking will kill us. A stake through the heart . . .'

'Don't be silly, Heather. You've been watching too many Dracula films.'

'I'm newer at this than you are . . . remember? Tell me, what *will* kill us?'

Moments passed before he answered.

'Daylight, not feeding, fire burns, water can drown us . . . We're not that much changed. We can't turn into bats or wolves or anything stupid like that. It's just that all our senses are heightened, more acute. That's what makes us stronger.'

But at what price?

I sighed. 'I still don't understand . . . what I am.'

Andrew got to his feet and pulled me up after him. 'Don't worry. Once you've got more used to it, you'll love it.'

'Do you?'

He looked straight at me but didn't answer.

Twenty-One

'So what do we do now that we've fed? Drift into some unsuspecting virgin's bedroom and make our presence felt? Howl at the moon? No, that's werewolves. How about if we . . . ?'

'How about if we go upstairs?'

All at once I became very still. Seconds ticked by.

'Why?'

'We have to make sure that your room is really secure from daylight.'

'Oh,' I said, relieved. 'How do we do that?'

'Newspaper over the windows stuck with sticky tape, then brown parcel paper over that ought to do it. I stuck the curtains down when you were out, but we need something more secure. Have you still got that roll of parcel paper in the kitchen?'

'Yes, but hang on. If I put newspaper over my windows, Mrs Tout will be over here in about two seconds flat.'

'Tell her you're repainting your window frames or something.'

I sighed again. 'All these lies – and it's going to get worse isn't it? We have to hide what we are and hide what we do. Hide, behind a mass of lies.'

'It's the only way. I don't like it any more than you do.'

I wondered.

'I don't think I'll ever get used to this.' The thoughts were spoken out loud before I could stop them spilling from my mouth.

'Yes you will.' He was confident. 'I promise.'

Half an hour later, my window was completely covered. There was no way a shaft of even the thinnest daylight could creep into my room. Andrew stood back, satisfied with what we'd done. It saddened me. It was like shutting out the rest of the world . . . or shutting ourselves in, away from it.

He came and stood behind me, wrapping his arms around my waist, kissing the back of my ear and nibbling on my earlobe.

'I can think of something else we can do now we're alone.'

'Don't, Andrew. Sex is the last thing on my mind at the moment. Besides, when you buggered off and left me in Fipoli, taking the pill wasn't exactly the top thing on my list. I haven't taken it since we arrived in Fipoli. We'll have to wait until after my next period. And anyway . . .' I shut up. If I went through all the excuses bubbling in my head, I'd be talking non-stop 'til morning.

'I'll wear a rubber. I'm sure there must be a chemist around here that's still open.'

'Andrew, I don't want to.'

His expression became guarded. 'Why not?'

'I need time.'

'You always need bloody time. For once in your life, can't you just do something and sod the consequences?'

'I thought I'd just done that,' I snapped back.

Silence.

'Sorry,' he said at last. 'I'll stop pushing. It's just that . . . that I do love you, Heather.'

'I know. I know.'

But for the first time I found myself wondering if love was really enough. Would it be enough to make this

126

work? I didn't know, and that scared me. I sat down on the bed.

'Andrew, are you sure you want us to live together?'

'We can't afford to live apart.' He sat down beside me.

'I guess not.'

Living with my boyfriend. Sleeping with my boyfriend. I felt old, *old*. I felt young, *young*.

'Where shall we live? It's not like we can go flat-hunting or get a mortgage or anything, is it?'

'We'll find something.' He shrugged. 'Maybe a house that's been abandoned. There are plenty of them in London.'

'But the council and all those private landlords lock them up. They even brick up the doors and windows.'

'So much the better. We can open up one window to get in and out by and the other bricked up doors and windows will keep everything and everyone else out.' He smiled.

'You make it all sound so simple.'

'It is. You're the one who says that things are only difficult if that's the way you make them.'

I stared into space. I'd got that saying from my dad. My face set into the usual unhappy frown which appeared whenever I thought of Dad. When he'd found out just how ill he was, he left us. Disappeared. Some stupid reason written in a letter and left by the phone. Something about not wanting to be a burden to us, not wanting us to watch him die.

I wish he hadn't done it. All those months lost. Months when we could have been together, and weren't. Dad came back home eventually, after Mum tracked him down, but we'd only had two months and one week and one day together after that. Even now I wasn't sure if I'd completely forgiven him for what he'd done. He'd taken the coward's way out, I'd thought at the time. It'd taken me ages to realise he'd done what he considered the brave thing, that he really did love us.

But still it hurt.

'Heather . . .' Andrew smiled. A smile that said he understood. I smiled back, gratefully. The Andrew I'd fallen in love with was in there still, somewhere. And I hadn't changed. Not the real me. This new thing, this was something I could deal with. I could handle it, control it. We both could. It didn't have to make that much difference. Not to the *real* us.

'We will make this work, won't we, Andrew?' I said fiercely.

'Of course we will. We can do anything. Don't you know that?'

I laughed, a strange, almost forgotten sound.

'We'll start looking for a place from tomorrow, and we'll find one.'

'Which leaves another big question? What're we going to tell our parents?'

'Yeah, I know. I was thinking about that too.' He frowned.

'And they're bound to want to see our new house, wherever it is.'

'They can't see it if we don't give them the address.'

I sighed again, long and hard. Mum would be hurt. How could I even begin to explain? Sorry, Mum, I can't live with you any more. But don't ask me where I'm going. I can't tell you. I could just see her face. A storm was going to erupt over that one.

'And what do we do for money?'

'I've got some saved.'

'So have I, but it won't last forever. We move one problem out of the way, only to be blocked by two more.'

'We'll manage. We just take it one day at a time.'

128

'That's not my style. You're a "take it as it comes" person. I like to plan my whole year in advance.'

'That's your problem,' Andrew teased.

'That depends on your point of view.' I wasn't in a teasing mood.

We sat in silence.

'Andrew . . . hold me,' I whispered at last. 'Suddenly, I need to be held very tight.'

We lay down on top of the bed and cuddled up, holding each other as if to let go for a moment would be to let go forever.

Over the next few days, I became slowly aware of how much my body was changing. Each evening as the sun set, Andrew and I woke up and, after a shower, we went hunting.

I could take very little *real* food. I'd tried to go without . . . feeding . . . but had been reduced to a wreck by the excruciating pain racking my body as a result. I didn't try again.

On the third night, I stopped feeling disgusted with myself. It hadn't taken very long.

But not just that, after each feed I felt weird. Strong and alert. It was as if there were nothing in the world I couldn't do. I heard conversations that were taking place streets away. I ran faster, jumped higher, knew I was stronger. It felt so strange, like growing away, apart from everyone else. I was different. *We* were different.

But I would have changed it all for one day of how things used to be. Not Andrew, though. With each passing hour, he grew more and more exultant. More and more contemptuous of what we had been before.

I wondered where it would end.

Twenty-Two

'Jessica, either eat it or leave it but don't play around with it.'

I smiled at Mum's words. I was at the top of our street, my whole body focused on our house. Mum and Jessica had finally come home. I couldn't wait to see them. I'd missed Mum so much. I'd even missed my scabby sister! I started to walk faster. After one night in Andrew's attic, already I longed for a proper bed with proper cotton sheets instead of a sleeping bag in a dusty, musty attic. We hadn't found a permanent place to stay yet. Andrew was surprised. I wasn't. The prospect of living indefinitely in the Harrison house made me more than a little anxious. Okay, they didn't know I . . . we were there, but surely it was only a matter of time until they did? Even so, I needed to take a break from house-hunting.

And as for the rest of our existence . . . I placed a hot hand to my even hotter cheeks. On leaving Andrew's attic tonight, we'd both gone to the park and fed on a stray dog. No more pets, I'd insisted. Only strays.

'So now we can both feel better about what we have to do, because really we're helping out the RSPCA!' Andrew scoffed, making me laugh reluctantly.

I'd wanted to feed before seeing Mum. My skin had been more ashen-grey than brown, before I fed, as if I'd soaked in the bath for a long time and not applied moisturiser to my skin afterwards. I knew Mum would pick up on something like that in a second.

'Mum, what time is Heather coming home?' I heard Jessica ask. I walked faster still.

'Don't know, love. All her note said was that she'd see us some time this evening.'

Now I could see that the downstairs lights were on. They looked welcoming.

'Where is she, then?' asked Jessica.

I opened our gate and headed towards the front door.

'She didn't say.'

I opened the door with my key. 'Mum, Jessica, I'm home.'

Mum came out of the living-room into the hall. I ran to her and hugged her, careful not to squeeze too tightly. Surprised at my enthusiasm, she hugged me back.

'I missed you, Mum.' I turned and hugged my sister. 'And you, you slimy ratbag!'

'Ratbag yourself!' Jessica wrinkled up her nose.

'So how was Ireland? I want to hear all about it.' One arm linked with Mum's, I put the other over Jessica's shoulder as we all went back into the living-room.

'It was okay. It would've been better if you'd been with us though.'

'Don't be nice to me, Jessica, I'm not used to it.' I grinned at her.

We all sat down around the table. Jessica and Mum were having chicken kiev, peas and baked potatoes for dinner.

'I didn't know what time you'd be back but I made plenty,' said Mum. 'Help yourself. It's on the hob.'

I stared at the chicken kiev on their plates. My insides felt as though they were being whisked. If I didn't move fast, I'd be sick all over the place.

'You didn't have to do that. I'm meeting Andrew in the Burger Bar later,' I mumbled.

'Oh I see.' Mum spoke quietly.

Opening my mouth was a mistake. The smell of the

chicken kiev filled my mouth and my nose and my eyes, making them water. I scrambled to my feet and went to sit on one of the armchairs, furthest away from the smell. When I looked up, Mum was frowning at me.

'Heather . . .'

'So tell me about your holiday,' I said, changing the subject quickly.

Jessica filled the gap and immediately started wittering. I could've kissed her!

We spent the next hour talking about their holiday. They asked me about mine. I gave edited highlights. Once or twice I caught Mum looking at me, a puzzled look on her face. She knew something wasn't quite right, I could never fool her for very long. After I'd helped with the washing-up, we sat down to watch telly. It was so peaceful, so comfortable – but it couldn't last.

'So where have you been today, Heather?' Mum asked quietly.

'Actually, I've been asleep for most of today.' At least that was the truth.

'Asleep? Where?'

'I was at Andrew's house. In a spare room.'

'During the day?' Mum's eyes narrowed, suspiciously. 'That's not like you. You're not ill, are you?'

I shook my head.

'Something's the matter. You're looking a bit peaky.'

'Mum, you're fussing.'

Stupidly, I risked a quick glance in her direction. A dawning light appeared in her eyes.

'Jessica, could you get me a glass of orange juice?' Mum said, never taking her eyes off me.

'But you've got a cup of tea by your feet,' protested Jessica.

'Then get one for yourself.'

'But I don't want one.'

'Jessica . . .'

132

'Oh, all right!' Jessica stood up, muttering. 'I bet you two are going to talk about boys and sex again! Why do I always get booted out at the good bits?'

'And don't listen at the door either,' Mum called out as Jessica left the room.

'Okay, Mum, spit it out.'

'Heather . . . are you pregnant?'

Shocked, I stared at her. 'No I am not! Give us a chance!'

I hadn't done anything to get pregnant yet! The days spent in my bed had been strictly for sleep and nothing else. I hadn't wanted to make love with Andrew. Not until we'd settled down to our new existence a bit more, and no way was I going to risk making any kind of noise in the Harrison's attic.

'Then what's wrong with you?'

I sought frantically for something to say. Something plausible.

'It's got something to do with Andrew, hasn't it? Has something happened between the two of you?'

I shook my head.

'You're lying,' Mum said instantly. 'I can always tell when you're lying. Something's wrong. And if you don't tell me the truth, I'm going to march straight round to Andrew's house and get the explanation from him.'

'You wouldn't!' I said, appalled. 'You wouldn't show me up like that.'

'In a hot New York second!' she replied.

It usually made me laugh when she said that. Not this time though, not this time.

'Listen, Mum, you wouldn't believe the truth if I told you,' I said desperately.

'Try me.'

I took a deep breath. 'Well, if you really want to know, Andrew was bitten at a party in Fipoli and he turned into a vam . . . a blood drinker and then he bit

133

me and now I'm the same. That's why I look a bit funny-peculiar.'

Mum's face became a mask. She drew herself up to her full height and her lips thinned.

'You're not amusing, Heather. Right, then, I get the point. You're seventeen and you're a woman, free to come and go as you please. And I should mind my own business, after all, I'm only your mother.'

'Mum, please . . .' I tried to touch her arm but she shrugged away from me.

That hurt.

'From now on I'll try to stay out of your life.' Her voice dripped with frost.

'I don't want you to stay out of my life. You're my mum,' I said impatiently.

'Then why don't you treat me like your mother and start acting like my daughter!' That stung. Silently, I counted to ten, my fingers outstretched.

'Mum, I don't want an argument. I really don't.' I sighed. 'And I'm fine, I promise.'

'We haven't even been back a day yet and already everyone's arguing. I'm sick of this.' Jessica was standing in the doorway, close to tears. How long had she been there? I looked at Mum. She looked at me.

'Sorry, Jessica. I'm sorry, Mum. Can't we . . . can't we just . . .'

'I'm sorry you ever set eyes on Andrew Harrison,' Mum mumbled.

I wasn't supposed to hear, but I did.

'Why don't you like him?' I asked unhappily.

'I've got nothing against Andrew . . .' Mum began.

'But? There was a but at the end of that.'

'But I've said too much already. As has been pointed out, it's none of my business.'

'Please, Mum. Why don't you like him?'

'Heather, I do like Andrew.' She sighed. 'I like him because he's obviously crazy about you.'

'But?'

'But you're both seventeen and . . .' She raised a hand when I would have interrupted. 'And no matter what you say, that is still too young to think about committing yourself to one person.'

'Why?'

'Because you don't know anything. You haven't done anything, you haven't seen anything of the world. If you get too serious now, you might regret it later. I just want to advise you, advise both of you, to slow down.'

For the very first time, I could hear what she was saying.

'What makes you think that Andrew and I are getting too serious?' I asked, lowering my gaze.

'I've got eyes. I can see how you feel about Andrew and it's no secret how he feels about you. Andrew feels things very deeply. He's very intense.'

'What's wrong with that?'

Mum shook her head. 'I know you, Heather. And I think I know Andrew. He wants to do new things, see new places, explore the world . . .'

'So do I.'

'Yes, but Andrew's happiest when he doesn't know what's going to happen tomorrow. And don't tell me you're the same, because you're not.' She continued quickly when I would have interrupted her. 'I doubt if you could walk to the bottom of our garden without mapping out your route back first.'

'You're being really unfair. I have been known to do things for the hell of it, or the fun of it, without needing an analytical breakdown first. I've even been known to do things for . . .'

Abruptly I stopped speaking.

'All I'm saying is be careful. Sooner or later one of you is going to get hurt. And I don't want that.'

'But you do like him?'

'Yes, Heather, I like him.' She smiled.

I smiled back at her.

'So what time will you be home tonight, if that's not being too nosy?'

My grin vanished. 'Mum, I'm coming to see you and Jessica tomorrow night and every night, but I . . . I can't sleep here any more.'

Mum became very still. 'And just where will you be staying? With Andrew?'

I nodded.

'At his house?'

'No, I only stayed there today. W-we have somewhere else to go to from tonight. A place of our own.'

'A place of . . . I see. And if I say I won't allow it, I suppose it'll do about as much good as forbidding you to go on holiday with Andrew.'

I didn't answer.

'Are you going to tell me where your new place is?'

'Well, er . . . it's not totally ours. What I mean is . . . we're sharing with one of Andrew's friends. Just until we get our own place.' I hated lying, I was so useless at it.

'And what are you going to use for money to pay for this place of your own?' fumed Mum.

'Andrew's sorting all that out.'

'Didn't you listen to a word I just said?' she asked, exasperated. 'Would it do any good to tell you you're both making a huge mistake?'

'You said you liked him,' I said angrily.

'But you didn't hear anything else I said, did you?'

'Yes I did. Mum, *please* . . .'

'Are you giving up school?' Mum asked icily.

'Of course not! I mean . . .'

136

Then I realised I couldn't go to school any more. I wouldn't be able to take my exams or go to university or get a job. They were all daytime activities. Ordinary daytime activities that I'd lost.

I walked over to the curtains and pulled them back. I looked up at the clear night sky, purple-blue, almost black. A dusting of silver stars twinkled down at me. The sunset must have been amazing.

Daytime activities.

'What do Andrew's parents think of all this?' Mum asked from behind me.

'I don't know. I haven't asked them. The same as you, I expect.'

'Heather, tell Andrew that you've changed your mind.'

'It's too late for that now.' I didn't realise I'd spoken out loud until I heard Mum's sharp intake of breath from behind me.

'Heather, what's going on?'

'Nothing.' I let the curtain fall back into place. 'I have to go now. I'll see you tomorrow.'

I was out of the room and by the front door before she had a chance to stop me.

'Heather, wait.' Jessica ran after me. 'Are you really leaving?'

I tried to smile and failed. 'Just 'cause I won't be living here any more doesn't mean you won't see me. I'll be round almost every day.'

'Then why go away?'

'I just have to, that's all.'

Jessica started to cry. No noise, no sniffling, just silent tears running down her cheeks. Mum came out of the living-room to stand in the hall. She didn't say a word.

'Oh, Jessica, please don't. You'll set me off in a minute.' I swallowed hard, past the choking lump in my throat. 'I won't be far away. I promise I'll never be far away.'

I bent to hug her close to me. After a few minutes hesitation, Jessica hugged me back, squeezing me.

'Heather, don't go,' she whispered.

'I have to,' I said unhappily. 'But I'll see you tomorrow, squirt, I promise.'

'Why are you going?' she sniffed.

'One day . . . maybe one day I'll tell you.' I sighed. 'I've got to go now. See you tomorrow. 'Bye Mum.'

I didn't hang around. I couldn't, I felt a right bitch.

''Bye Mum,' I said again, closing the door behind me.

I walked quickly up the street. I needn't have worried, the front door didn't open. I was half-way up the street when the sound of Mum's voice stopped me in my tracks.

'Oh Heather . . . Heather, I hope you know what you're doing.'

I turned my head. There was no one behind me. Then I realised that she was still indoors. I covered my ears with my hands and started to run.

Twenty-Three

'Heather, you've arrived just in time.' Diane beckoned me over the moment I entered the Burger Bar.

Andrew, Diane, Pete, Vijay, Ben, Caroline, they were all there. I forced a smile and waved and walked over to them, hoping I didn't look as dejected as I felt. I passed by a baby in a pushchair on my way to my friends' table. She was so cute, dressed in pink and with the longest eyelashes I'd ever seen on any infant. I stopped walking.

You have your whole life ahead of you, I thought. For you anything is possible and maybe even probable.

But the baby took one look at me and started howling. I hurried on, feeling the parents' glaring eyes boring into my back.

When I reached my friends' table, Andrew smiled at me sympathetically. He and Pete were seated on the same long bench, separated by Caroline and Ben. There was still frost between them, not surprising after their last encounter.

'What's happening?' I asked, sliding into the booth next to Diane.

'We want you to settle an argument. We're voting on who's the best wind-up merchant at this table.' Diane laughed.

'Oh, that's easy.' I grinned. 'Pete Shorman wins that one, hands down.'

'I told you!' Pete took a mock bow.

'What're you talking about? I'm better at winding people up than Pete,' Vijay scorned.

'And I'm the best,' said Caroline.

'Nope. Pete beats you all. Listen to this. Pete told me that he didn't stand me up on our first date. He said he asked Andrew to give me the message that he couldn't make it. Only Andrew decided not to give me that message, but take me out himself instead. And do you know something, Pete actually had me believing it for a couple of micro-seconds.'

I creased up laughing at the memory, but my laughter died when I realised I was the only one at the table enjoying the joke. Diane was making all kinds of faces in my direction. Vijay and Ben were looking at the décor on the wall behind them. Caroline was having a coughing fit. Pete was looking into his mineral water as if a goldfish had just appeared in it.

And Andrew's face was a mask as he regarded Pete.

'What's the matter? Don't you lot think that's funny?' I asked, puzzled.

Diane kicked me under the table. 'Oh sorry, my foot slipped.'

I looked across at Andrew. He was still watching Pete. Pete straightened up to look straight back at him. It was as though there were a silent conversation flowing between them.

And I understood every word.

Pete *had* been telling me the truth! It hadn't been a wind-up at all. And everyone had known except me. God, how could I have been so slow!

'Oh Andrew.' I could think of nothing else to say.

'Thanks a lot, Pete,' Andrew said quietly. He wasn't even going to try and deny it.

'Listen, Andrew, I told Heather I was just joking. You're the one who's just admitted to her that it was all true.'

'You said you wouldn't say anything to her at all.' Andrew's voice was getting quieter and quieter.

'I only told her because it looked like you two might be splitting up.'

'So you thought you'd make sure of it.'

'I told her I was joking, remember.'

'Don't you two dare talk around me as if I'm not here,' I said furiously.

They looked at me briefly before turning back to each other.

'I'll remember this, Pete,' Andrew said softly.

Pete held out his hand and shook it. 'I'm trembling, Andrew,' he replied scornfully.

'Come on, you two. Can we change the subject please?' Diane asked. 'Pretty please!'

Pete turned back to his drink, Andrew looked at me, I looked at him. It was the expression on his face that did it. For the first time, I was frightened. Not anxious. Not nervous. Frightened.

Of Andrew.

Twenty-Four

Everyone did their best to lighten the mood around our table, but it was no good. I didn't feel like speaking. Neither did Andrew. Neither did Pete. After five minutes of listening to the others struggle to make bright conversation, I stood up.

'You're not leaving, are you?' Diane said dismayed.

Andrew stood up as well.

'Yeah, I think so. It's time I was going.'

'It's time we were *both* going,' Andrew amended, moving past Ben and Caroline. 'Excuse me, Pete.'

Without a word, Pete swung his legs around to let Andrew pass. Andrew and I walked out of the Burger Bar together, but apart. We were half-way up the road before Andrew spoke.

'Aren't you going to talk to me?'

'What would you like me to say?'

'Heather, please.'

I stopped walking and turned to him. 'What you did was the meanest, sneakiest, most underhand thing I've ever heard of. I thought you and Pete were friends.'

'We are . . . we were.' Andrew spoke bitterly. 'Until he told you what really happened.'

I couldn't believe his attitude.

'Pete's telling me isn't the issue. Surely the point here is what you did?' I said with sarcasm.

'I had to. You would never have given me a second look otherwise.'

'Rubbish. All you had to do was sit down and talk to me.'

'That's not true, and you know it. I know how you felt about me. I was a prize lemon. A dork.'

'Only 'cause in the last couple of years every time I tried to talk to you, you'd answer in monosyllables and then scoot off. I thought you considered yourself too great to talk to me.'

'That's because I could never think of anything to say.'

'You managed okay when you took Pete's place,' I pointed out, coldly.

'I didn't have any choice. It was then, or never. You were going out with Pete, remember. I knew I didn't stand much of a chance once you two became an item., And I thought . . . all's fair . . . and all that.'

'No, it isn't. What you did was wrong.'

'I know. After a while I managed to persuade Pete that he shouldn't say anything unless you and I split up.'

'And just how did you manage that?'

'He could see I was serious about you. And you seemed to like me. We started seeing each other regularly. So I asked him not to say anything to break us up and he didn't, until now . . .'

'Andrew . . .' I shut up. I couldn't be bothered to argue. He couldn't see past the fact that Pete had told me the truth. We carried on walking.

'Do you wish Pete had turned up at that cinema rather than me?'

I looked at him, but he was looking straight ahead. 'It doesn't make much difference now, does it? You're the one I'm going out with. You're the one I went on holiday with.'

'Are you sorry?'

I didn't answer. I couldn't answer.

'I see.'

'I can't understand what made you do it. It's not like

you. It's not the Andrew *I* know.' I spoke more to myself than Andrew. I looked at him. 'It makes me wonder which Andrew is the real one.'

'The one walking next to you. And I didn't lie to you. You just assumed I'd been stood up.'

'You lied by omission which is just the same. Don't play word games with me. I'm not doing an A level in English Lit for nothing!'

Five minutes passed before either of us spoke again.

'So what happens now?' Andrew asked. 'Do we go on looking for somewhere of our own so we can live together, do we go back to my house, do we . . .? What?'

'I don't honestly know. My head is spinning. I . . . I need to be alone for a while. I need time to think.'

'About what?'

'About things.' I couldn't say any more than that.

'So where are you going? Home?'

'I can't. I told Mum I was living with you. And she'd only ask a ton of questions.'

'I'm sorry.'

That word again.

Sorry doesn't help, I thought with sudden anger. Sorry is worth bugger all.

A woman walking her Alsatian dog approached us. Within feet of us the dog bared its teeth and began to growl. Andrew and I stopped walking and watched it. The dog began to bark vigorously, its ears pointing straight back, its hair bristling.

'Roxanne!' the woman admonished. 'Roxanne, behave!'

As I watched I was aware that for the first time I wasn't the least bit scared of the snarling brute. Usually a dog only had to look at me askance to send me speeding in the opposite direction. I could see that the dog wasn't being particularly aggressive or hostile. It was more scared than anything else.

'If you don't shut up, you could end up as our dinner . . .' Andrew mumbled so that only I could hear him. I elbowed him in the ribs.

'I'm so sorry,' the woman smiled. 'I can't think what has got into her. She isn't usually like this.'

Andrew and I smiled back. The woman had practically to pull her dog past us. Roxanne never took her eyes off us until she was well out of our way.

'Andrew and Heather Services Limited. All babies and animals love us!' Andrew said sardonically.

'The cheapest babysitting rates in town. Dark nights only. Daytime work cannot be considered.' I smiled.

'Apply to the Harrison attic.'

'Until further notice!'

We started laughing. It didn't last long.

'It feels like we haven't done that in a while,' Andrew said what I was thinking.

'We used to laugh all the time,' I remembered.

'We haven't had so much to laugh about recently.'

We looked at each other.

'I'll see you tomorrow night.'

'Tomorrow? Where are you going to sleep?' He wasn't happy – to say the least.

'I don't know. I just want to walk for a while. To be honest, I don't feel like company. I have some thinking to do. I'll find somewhere, don't worry.'

'Like where?'

'I'll find something. I need to be alone.'

'I see. And tomorrow?'

'I'll worry about that when it gets here. Isn't it about time I adopted your policy?'

Not knowing what else to say, I turned away.

'Heather . . .'

I looked round.

'I know what you're doing, I'm not stupid. I should have given you Pete's message. I knew that then, and I know it now. But I'll tell you something, if I had to do it all over again, I wouldn't change a thing. Not a thing.'

And with that he turned and walked away from me, leaving me to watch him.

Twenty-Five

I woke up the following evening shivering from cold and hunger. The previous night I'd walked and walked. A wild thought about greeting the sunrise had even entered my head.

But then I'd thought of Mum and Jessica and Andrew . . . and myself, and I couldn't do it. I'd never been a coward, and I wasn't about to change now, but guilt gnawed away at me like a starving dog with a bone.

I'd been too angry to let Pete explain about our broken date; I should never have accepted the drinks Julius gave us; I'd hurt Mum and upset Jessica. My life was a mess and, like a contagious disease, it seemed to be infecting all those around me.

At first all I could think about was how Andrew had lied to me and cheated Pete. Maybe I should've been flattered by what he did, but I wasn't.

But no, in the end, I wasn't sorry I'd gone out with Andrew. And after just one night away from him, I knew I never would be. I'd needed the time alone though, I couldn't think straight with him near me. It was being with him that confused me. Now at least I'd finally worked things out. I knew how I felt about me and Andrew.

I loved him, and he loved me. And maybe, when you got right down to it, that *was* all that really mattered. The rest would take care of itself if we could just get that right.

My trouble was that I was always looking backwards,

not forwards. But no more of that. It was time to accept things as they were. Andrew wasn't perfect. Neither was I.

And we *were* blood drinkers, destined to each other. We had to drink to survive. We had no choice. And we had to do our living by night. I'd never see the sun again, or a blue sky or a white cloud and that made something inside of me ache ... but it was time to accept that fact and move on, with Andrew.

We'd find a place of our own. Somewhere where we could be together, a place to call home. And I could still study, by correspondence classes or maybe the Open University.

There are always ways, I told myself, always alternatives. It would work out, if we really wanted it to, if we fought hard enough to make sure it did. That's what Dad always said. I realised now that he too had found the words and the actual deeds difficult to reconcile. That's why I'd never really forgiven him. He'd always said one thing, then done another. It'd taken me until last night finally to realise it. Dad and I were a lot alike! Maybe too much alike, but I was determined to get it right. It hadn't taken me as long as it'd taken Dad to sort myself out. He'd have been proud of me.

However, my first priority was to get out of this derelict office block, where I'd spent the day and feed. Sleeping alone hadn't been much fun either. I'd go to Mum's and have a shower. Then I'd find Andrew. Suddenly I knew what I was doing and where I was going. It was a wonderful feeling.

What would he say when I told him how I felt? Would he feel the same? Would he agree with me? Or would he be so sick of my moods that he wouldn't care? No, I couldn't believe that. I remembered the way he looked when I told him I wanted to be alone. He loved me. And I did feel better. Andrew and I would be fine, we'd be better than fine. What was the saying? Today was the first day of the rest of our lives.

'Hello, Caroline. Hi, Ben. Has either of you seen Andrew?' Ben and Caroline were alone in our gang's usual booth and they didn't welcome the interruption. Tough!

'Hi, Heather. Er . . . he was in here briefly about half an hour ago,' Ben replied.

'Do you know where he went?'

'No idea,' Caroline said. 'He and Pete had a brief conversation and then they left together.'

'They left together?'

Caroline and Ben nodded. I didn't know what to make of that. Maybe Pete and Andrew had made up? I hoped so. They'd been good friends before. So why did I feel uneasy . . . ?

After all, why shouldn't they leave together? What had happened all those months ago was now just water under the bridge.

'Oh, all right. Thanks anyway. I'll leave you two to it then.'

Ben and Caroline didn't argue for me to stay. I left the Burger Bar trying to summon up the courage to visit the Harrison household.

You should eat first. Face Mrs Harrison on a full stomach at least! I thought.

I turned to walk to Andrew's house. A gentle breeze whispered across my face. It carried the faintest scent of blood in it. Fresh, sweet blood. My mouth filled with saliva. My stomach rumbled hungrily. Licking my lips, I stood perfectly still and sniffed. Now that I was concentrating on the smell, it was stronger.

The aroma came from the darkened alley-way beside the Burger Bar. Gingerly I began to walk up it, picking my way through the mounds of burger cartons and split

149

black bin-liners. There was no light in the alley, except that which filtered through the frosted glass windows at the side of the restaurant. I concentrated on seeing through the darkness. The smell was getting stronger all the time. Pungent. I licked my lips. Even though I'd already fed on two cats I'd found in the derelict office block, the smell still made me feel hungry. Then I saw him. Pete.

Sprawled on the ground on top of a pile of rotting, stinking rubbish. The tiniest pool of blood had collected under his slightly open lips. My hands flew to my mouth. Pete stared with unseeing eyes at the wall in front of him. I strained to hear a heartbeat but there was none, there was no sound at all. Just the rumble of the traffic on the main road and the clatter of pans and pots from the Burger Bar kitchen. My breath caught in my throat. I didn't need to get any closer to see that Pete was dead.

He was dead.

My mind wanted me to scream and to vomit. I couldn't get the smell of blood out of my nostrils. It hung in the air, surrounding me. I could almost taste it.

Pete . . .

Footsteps approached. I looked around. It was a dead-end. I mustn't be found here, there would be questions. Questions which would last through the night, and well into daylight . . .

Opposite the restaurant was a wall, four metres high. Without hesitation I bent my knees and leapt to the top of it. Had I stopped to think about it I never would've done it. The footsteps were nearer. I turned to see who it was. A woman and a man who worked at the restaurant, each carrying a large black bin-liner.

'If that woman says one more thing to me . . .'

'You've got more patience than I have,' the woman's companion said sympathetically.

'Patience! It's not patience. If I didn't need this job . . . Dave . . . ? Dave, what's that?'

'What? I don't see anything.'

'Over there. By the far wall.'

Gingerly they walked forward, almost on tip-toe.

'Karen, someone's there,' Dave whispered.

'Oh, I see now. Leave him. He's probably drunk or something,' Karen replied with distaste. She and Dave carried on moving slowly forwards.

'I . . . I don't think so. He doesn't look too good . . .'

'Is he okay?' Karen whispered. Then they reached Pete.

'Oh my God! Look!' And Karen screamed. I didn't wait to hear any more. I straightened up and ran along the narrow wall.

It had to have been Andrew. It had to be him. But why? *Why?* He had no reason to do that to Pete.

Yesterday when I'd learnt the truth about my non-existent first date with Pete, I'd seen the look in Andrew's eyes as he looked at Pete. And now Pete was dead. Oh God! *Pete was dead.*

And Andrew had killed him. Because he was stronger, because he could. I should have been there to stop him, but I'd been away feeling sorry for myself, thinking only about myself. To think I used to love it when Andrew was jealous. How naive! How stupid, stupid, stupid! *And now Pete was dead.*

And Andrew was a killer. I had to find him. I couldn't rest until I found him. I wanted to cry . . . but I couldn't. Sand burned my eyes and filled my throat and I felt sick. Sick because I hadn't been sick. What had I turned into? What had we both turned into?

Something vile and rotten and repulsive. Something no longer human. Not the super humans Andrew said

151

we were, but something less than that. *Much less than that!*

And I had to do something about it.

Twenty-Six

'Oh it's you.' Mrs Harrison's face fell. 'What do you want?'

'Is Andrew in?'

I had no time to be pleasant to this unpleasant woman. I'd run all the way from the Burger Bar and I'd already been around the back of the house and up to the attic but Andrew wasn't there. I was *burning* to find him. I kept thinking about the way Pete had looked when I discovered his body. He hadn't deserved that, no one deserved that. I would find Andrew if it took me all night.

'You know more about his whereabouts than I do,' Mrs Harrison said bitterly.

'I don't understand.'

'You heard me. Ever since he took up with you I've hardly seen him. And now he's moved right out. I hope you're satisfied.'

'Is he here now?' I repeated impatiently.

'He might have come home and gone straight up to his room when I was in the sitting-room. He barely talks to me these days. That's something else I can thank you for.'

'D'you mind if I check.' I stepped past her before she could stop me. I didn't give a toss whether she minded or not.

'Well, really!'

'Andrew!' I shouted out from the hall.

Mrs Harrison closed the front door before turning to face me. 'Do you have to shout like a common fishwife?'

'How would you like me to shout then?'

'Must you shout at all?'

'ANDREW! Are you up there?' I yelled even louder. Mrs Harrison closed her eyes as if in pain.

'ANDREW!' I turned back to Mrs Harrison just in time to see the look of disgust on her face.

'Don't you look at me like that, you stuck-up snob. And I've never seen anyone who had less to be snobbish about!'

'I'll never know what my son sees in you.' Mrs Harrison shook her head. 'Novelty value no doubt. I can only pray that the novelty will wear off soon.'

I stretched out my fingers. I didn't need this. Not now. Not tonight.

'Or maybe he wanted someone who was as different from his mother as he could get.' I tried to keep my voice even.

Andrew, you didn't have to do that . . . You didn't have to . . .

'Now that you know Andrew isn't here, please leave.' Her eyes narrowed.

'Listen, Mrs Harrison, I know you don't like me and that's fine 'cause I don't like you either,' I said quietly, my fingers stretched to the point of breaking.

'At least that's something we both agree on,' Mrs Harrison muttered under her breath.

Every word rang in my ears like a bell. I glared at her.

'It doesn't matter what I say or do, does it? And it never will,' I said quietly. 'You can't get past the fact that I'm black. You're not the slightest bit interested in who I am or what I think and feel. I'm black and that's what you can't forgive. Well, here's a hot news flash, I'm proud of what I am. I wouldn't change even if I could. So stuff you!'

154

'How dare you?' Her face turned puce. She wasn't the only one drowning in fury at that moment.

'Easy. I'm sick of you and your snotty attitude. You're no better than anyone else, Mrs Harrison, you just think you are. It's thanks to you that both your sons think they can do what they like and get away with it. They both think their opinions are more valid than anyone else's. They both think they can do whatever they like with impunity. Your whole family makes me sick.'

With a start, I realised what I'd said, about *both* her sons. I hadn't meant to say that, the words had just slipped out of my mouth. Was that what I really believed? And then I knew it wasn't a question of what I wanted to believe any more. It was just the truth. Even Andrew – my Andrew – was as arrogant as his mother. In his own way.

'Get out of my house.' Mrs Harrison moved towards me.

'With pleasure. I regret ever setting foot in this mausoleum.'

'I'm sure that makes two of us.'

Something . . . say something to hurt her, the way she's hurt you, I told myself. Something . . .

'Yeah, but I'm sure I'm not the only one who can't stand this house. Andrew couldn't wait to leave here and live with me, Morgan spends as much time away from this place as possible, and Mr Harrison seems to spend a lot of nights elsewhere. He can't be working late *every* night.'

Before either of us could think about it, Mrs Harrison raised her hand high and slapped my face. I could see each movement frame by frame as it came, but I was rooted to the spot. As if I couldn't believe, *wouldn't* believe that she would really do it. But she did.

I scowled at her. My temper flew out the window.

'Why, you . . .'

I raised my hand and slapped her back. The force of my slap lifted her off her feet and sent her sailing through the air. I watched horror-stricken as Mrs Harrison hit the banisters side on. Her head hit the balustrade with a sickening thud. She crumpled up and fell to the ground like a wet rag.

And there it was, the smell of blood again.

Blood. Blood, blood bloodbloodblood . . .

Twenty-Seven

I ran over to her and crouched down. Her eyes were closed but she was still breathing. I picked up her hand by the wrist to feel for a pulse. The sound of the front door opening sent my head whipping around. Morgan and Andrew stood in the doorway. We all froze.

'What the hell . . . ?'

Morgan was the first to break the spell.

I looked down at Mrs Harrison. I was still holding her hand. I dropped it immediately and stood up.

'Andrew, it's . . .'

'You bitch!' Morgan ran over to his mother, pushing me aside.

'Andrew,' I stepped forward. 'I . . . it's not what you think . . .'

One look at Andrew's face and everything I wanted to say died in my mouth. He stared at me with disbelief. And as I watched, disbelief turned to anger and anger turned into something much, much worse.

'Andrew, it was an accident,' I whispered. 'She . . . I . . .'

'Andrew, phone for an ambulance,' Morgan said urgently. 'Mum's still alive but her pulse is weak.'

Andrew didn't move. He didn't take his eyes off me.

'For heaven's sake, Andrew,' Morgan said with fury. 'We'll deal with her later. Right now, we have to get Mum to hospital. Fast.'

When Andrew still didn't move, Morgan swore and reached across for the phone on the telephone table. I took a step towards Mrs Harrison. I only wanted to help. I knew some first-aid. Morgan tensed. Andrew moved to grab my arm.

'Don't you go near her. *Don't you touch her*,' he hissed at me.

'I was only trying . . .'

'I know what you were trying to do,' Andrew said.

'The same thing that you did to Pete?'

What I'd meant as a question came out as a rationale, an excuse. I hadn't meant it like that at all. But from Andrew's face I could see that he'd misunderstood me.

'So you thought you'd get even,' Andrew said softly. 'Why wasn't I listening for you? I should have known . . . I should have been listening . . .' The harshness of his voice made me flinch. Behind me I could hear Morgan talking to the emergency services.

'It wasn't like that. It . . . it was an accident.'

'Yeah, of course it was,' Morgan interrupted, his hand over the mouthpiece of the phone.

I turned to him. 'Yes it was. I swear . . .'

'Don't listen to her, Andrew,' Morgan said fiercely. His attention returned to the phone in his hand.

I looked down at Mrs Harrison but all I could see was Pete. I tried to think of Pete but all I could see was Mrs Harrison. I was going crazy. The whole world was turning upside down and tipping me with it. I turned back to Andrew.

'Pete . . . Andrew, why did you do it? Pete was harmless. How could you . . . ?'

'He deserved it.' Andrew's voice was ice cold, ice hard. 'He's the reason you left me. He split us up. Only now I see that you weren't worth it.'

I flinched as though Andrew had struck me.

'So what you did doesn't matter? The only thing that counts is what you think I did to your mother? Is that . . . ?'

'I was angry,' Andrew shouted. 'Pete and I were

158

quarrelling and I forgot what I was, and punched him. You were out for revenge. That's the difference.'

No difference at all, I thought stunned. *No difference at all*.

'Listen, Andrew . . .'

'No, I won't listen. Not any more.'

I'd never seen Andrew like this before. I'd never seen that look on his face. Morgan put the phone down and cradled his mum's head in his lap.

'I know what you are,' Morgan said to me. 'Andrew told me everything on the way back from the Burger Bar. But don't think that being a vampire is going to protect you. I'm going to spend each and every day from now on hunting you until I find you. And I *will* find you.'

'I'm not scared of you, Morgan.' I swallowed hard.

'You should be,' he replied slowly. He turned to Andrew. 'Andrew, I think you should make me the same as you. She wouldn't stand a chance against both of us.'

'Don't worry, Morgan. Heather's my problem.'

I looked at Andrew. He looked at me.

'Okay, Heather, if that's the way you want it . . .' he told me ominously.

I looked around. Mrs Harrison was unconscious. Morgan would stop at nothing now to get me. And as for Andrew . . . Andrew was a stranger. A dangerous stranger. Everything was closing in on me. The walls. Morgan. Andrew. What I was. What I'd become. So I fled. I bolted for the front door and flung it open and ran.

'No, Andrew, don't go after her. I know how we can get her to come to us . . .' I heard Morgan say.

I kept running. A slight drizzle began to fall. The moon was hidden behind a thick blanket of dark clouds.

159

I ran faster and faster until the people I passed in the street could only feel me as a rush of air racing by them.

And I was crying. I wiped my hands across my face and was surprised, then not surprised, to see blood. No more salt-water tears. Just tears of blood.

I didn't know where I was running to. Where could I go? Back to the derelict office block? Andrew might find me there. All he'd have to do was wander around and concentrate on hearing my breathing or smelling my perfume or listening for the sound of my crying. *I had to keep moving.* I didn't dare stop, at least not until I was closer to the dawn than I had yet been. Only then could I be reasonably certain that Andrew would be more concerned about finding shelter for the day than finding me. But that would still leave Morgan . . .

I kept running and walking, and hiding at every muted sound that might be Andrew. I wondered how Mrs Harrison was doing; in spite of everything I hoped she was all right. Never again would I forget how strong I was.

And how was my mum doing? I'd told her I would see her but I didn't dare risk it. Maybe Morgan and Andrew were watching her house, expecting me to turn up there sooner or later. I wasn't going to let Mum or Jessica get involved in all this. I had to find a way out of this one myself. One thing was for sure, Andrew and Morgan wouldn't rest until they found me.

Would Andrew make Morgan a blood drinker as Morgan requested? Would I have at least one day's grace before I had to face them both? If that was the case then maybe I could go and see my family.

I walked until I found myself outside Diane's house. It was early morning now, a couple of hours before dawn. The street was dimly lit by the street lamps. The silence around me was deafening. Only two of the houses in the street still had their lights on. Diane's house was in darkness, but I knew her bedroom was at the back. After making sure that there was no one else around, I jumped the side gate and walked up the path to the back garden. I stood there, thinking.

Maybe I could make Diane a drinker, the same as me. Then I wouldn't be alone, then I'd have someone else on my side. I wouldn't wake her up, though. If I drank just enough blood to knock her out then I could take her somewhere safe and make her the same.

If Andrew could do it, why not me? I could get in through her window easily. All I had to do was jump up on to the kitchen window-sill and then spring up to her open window. Diane would join me. I knew she would. We were friends.

I hung my head.

'How could you?' I whispered.

Diane and I *were* friends. So was I really going to drag her in to my miserable life sentence? For the first time it struck me how alone I was. Really alone. This wasn't living. I was struggling just to stay alive. God, how I missed the daylight. How I missed sunshine on my face. Did I really want this for my friend too?

'Sorry, Diane.' I spoke up to her window.

I walked down the side path and, once out in the street, I started to run. Again.

Twenty-Eight

It took me an hour of walking to decide what to do next. It was so logical I wondered why I hadn't thought of it sooner. But I needed some things first. I travelled all the way into town to find a twenty-four-hour supermarket which sold writing pads and envelopes. Glancing down at my watch I realised that I didn't have much time left before the sun rose. The minutes were running faster than I was. And I was getting dizzy.

I knew I needed to feed some more but I couldn't face it. Not tonight. Not after so much blood had already been spilt. I knew what I was doing was dangerous − I might not wake up the next evening − but the thought of drinking again that night . . .

Hopping on to a night bus, I sat in the rear seat upstairs, as far away from the two other people on the bus as I could get. For the first time I wasn't sure if I trusted myself. The need to drink was getting worse. And lone people were easier to find than stray animals. The fact that I could even think like that sickened me. How long would it be before I had no choice but to feed on people? Or maybe I would have a choice and just wouldn't care any more.

'Never,' I told myself fiercely. 'You'll never do that.'

As I sat back in my seat, I forced myself to calm down and think properly. When Mrs Harrison had been knocked out . . . when I'd knocked her out, she'd been badly injured. I saw that at once. So the chances were that Morgan and Andrew hadn't been out looking for me at all. They were probably both in the local hospital

162

with their mother still. I hoped fervently that they were, I couldn't deliver my letter otherwise. I felt sure I was right. Morgan and Andrew would be too busy with their mother to think about me. There was always tomorrow for that . . . And the next day, and the day after that.

I dug a pen out of my pocket and started to write.

Dear Andrew,
I've decided that

I scrunched up the piece of paper and threw it on the floor. I started again.

Andrew,
I've decided that the best thing for both of us is for
me to go away, far away. Please believe me, I didn't
mean to hurt your mum. We had ~~an argument~~ a
quarrel and I lost my temper and slapped her. I forgot
how strong ~~I am~~ we are. That's the truth, I swear it
is. I hope with all my heart she gets better.
Heather.
P.S. You had no reason to do what you did to Pete.
He hadn't split us up. I was trying to find you to tell
you that, but I always did have lousy timing.

I folded up the letter and put it in an envelope.

Fifteen minutes later the bus stopped as close to Andrew's house as it was ever going to get. I got off and stood still for a few moments. Even being this near his house made me nervous. What if I was wrong and he was at home?

'Come on, Heather. You're not a coward,' I whispered to myself, then immediately wished I hadn't. If Andrew was anywhere within the next few streets, with his hearing, he was bound to have heard that. I stood

163

still and listened. I could hear nothing out of the ordinary. So early in the morning there was barely anything to hear. I started walking.

Once I reached Andrew's street, I entered the garden via a side gate of the first house I came to. I'd have more cover if I approached his house from the back rather than from the road. When I reached the Harrison garden I was perspiring, not from exertion but from fear. I jumped on to the conservatory roof as quietly as I could but still I made a slight noise. I froze for countless seconds. Nothing. Shaking, I jumped up on to the roof and froze. If Andrew were in the attic he must have heard me.

There was no sound, no movement from within. Ducking low, I ran across the sloping roof to the skylight. It was open. That usually meant that Andrew wasn't home. When I'd been in the attic, Andrew closed it only when we were ready to settle down for the day. He'd covered the skylight from the inside with a thick, midnight-blue, velvet curtain that his mum used to keep in a drawer. No light could penetrate that but, as a precaution, Andrew and I still had placed our sleeping-bags in the darkest corner of the attic, as far away from the skylight as we could get.

So this was it. If the open skylight was a trick to get me into the attic then I was about to fall for it. Opening it slightly wider I took a deep breath and jumped down. I immediately expected Andrew to grab my arms, with Morgan there to help him. Silence. I was alone.

Almost crying with relief, I went over to Andrew's sleeping-bag. I wasn't going to hang around waiting for him to come back. Placing the letter where he couldn't help but see it, I headed back for the skylight. I jumped out, then paused on the roof. Apart from a cat mewing, several houses away, and the breath of the wind, there was no sound.

I leapt down from the roof, straight in to the garden.
I was winded slightly on impact but that was all. Closing
my eyes, I allowed myself to drift away for a few
moments. Only the moments turned into minutes and
I lost all track of time. I tried to decide what to do next
but my mind was blank. With a sigh I opened my eyes
and jumped over the fence into next door's garden.
Then I heard it, the sound of footsteps. One set almost
indiscernible, the other heavy. I froze.

'Don't worry, I'll find her,' said Morgan.

'Morgan, you're not to do anything without me.'

'You think I'm afraid of her? I don't care if she is a
vampire. She could be a vampire and a werewolf com-
bined and I'd still get her!'

'No you wouldn't. She's far stronger than you are.
She's as strong as me now. My only threat.'

'Then why don't you make me one too?'

'We've been over this before,' Andrew sighed.
'Making Heather the same as me was a mistake. And I
don't repeat mistakes.'

'But I want you to . . .'

'No! That's final.'

There was a moment's pause as they opened the side
gate, closing it behind them.

'I wouldn't have believed any of this if I hadn't seen
what you did to that black bloke,' Morgan said.

'I'm sorry I did that. I shouldn't have lost my temper
and hit him. Oh hell! I . . . I heard his neck snap. He
didn't stand a chance.' I heard Andrew shake his head.

'What's done is done,' Morgan dismissed him. 'The
point is, what are you going to do now?'

'I'll find Heather. Don't worry.' Andrew's tone chilled
my blood. And still I didn't dare breathe.

'And when you find her?'

There was no reply.

'Just don't forget, little brother, that she tried to kill

our mother. You know how we found her, bent over Mum's wrist, ready to drink her blood.'

'I'm not likely to forget, am I?'

'And you know what the doctor at the hospital said . . .'

'Morgan, I did hear him. My ears work, thank you.'

'Well, I know you. All Heather would have to do is tell you some cock-and-bull story about it being an accident and you'd believe her.'

'Not this time. Don't worry, Morgan. I know better now,' Andrew said softly. 'Heather is dangerous.'

'Too right. We've got to make sure that she doesn't get to Mum or any of us, ever again.'

Andrew took a deep breath. 'I know . . . I shouldn't have changed her. I shouldn't have made her the same as me. I had no right.'

'You didn't hold a gun to her head,' Morgan scoffed. 'It was her choice. I bet she couldn't wait. It was her chance to get back at Mum and Dad and me . . .'

'It wasn't like that.'

'There you go again, defending her,' Morgan said furiously.

'Drop it, Morgan. And I mean it. You're not to do anything until I wake up tomorrow evening. We'll find her together.'

'And make her pay.'

Andrew didn't answer. He didn't have to.

I listened as he sprung up on to the conservatory roof. I drew back into the shadow of the fence, praying that he wouldn't turn around and see me. Morgan lifted up the loose brick which hid the key to the conservatory door and let himself in to the house. Even then I only dared to let out my breath a little at a time. I had to get out of here. Fast.

I had to get out of this. There had to be a way.

Then it hit me. Julius . . . The only place to get any

166

answers was in Fipoli. Julius was the only one who could help Andrew and me now.

He was my only hope.

Twenty-Nine

It took six nights of travelling to make it to Fipoli. Having to find safe places to spend my days had slowed me right down. I didn't take much with me, just a sleeping-bag with some dirt from my back garden in a polythene bag at the bottom of it, and more dirt beneath the inner soles of my shoes.

I wasn't going to give up. I knew what I wanted now. It was simple. I wanted to be changed back into a normal person, in to a boringly ordinary individual again. Once I'd returned to normal, maybe I could persuade Andrew to follow me. Now that he'd had time to calm down and think, he must have realised that I wasn't his enemy. What had he called me? A threat? What a laugh!

Once I was normal, Andrew would remember how things used to be between us. Surely, like me, he wanted that back? Everything else was lies and talk. If he could revert to human, he would. I was convinced of it.

And if he didn't . . .

I shook my head, refusing to speculate in that direction. All I had to do was convince Andrew that what had happened with his mother had been an accident. A way back for both of us was something to be seized with eager open arms. But first things first.

To find Julius.

I came upon Fipoli from the northern route. It felt strange to see it again, after what seemed like years rather than a few weeks. The whitewashed buildings

168

with their coloured shutters seemed like something from another world.

It was almost five o'clock in the morning and the streets were deserted. Not just empty but deserted. Not a dog, not a cat, not a tramp. Nothing. I made my way to the main street running through Fipoli town centre. I knew my way, and I didn't have much time. The dawn was approaching fast. I'd cut the last part of my journey very fine.

Within two or three minutes of finding the main street, I was at Julius' house. I'd only fed lightly, so all the exertion made me hungry, but I wasn't going to feed. Not now. Not when I was so *close*. I strode up to the front door and knocked. Now that I was here I was impatient to see him. He had to be able to help me. He just had to.

After what seemed like ages, the door opened slowly. Julius stood there, shrouded in shadows. At the sight of him, my heartbeat raced. This was it. Would he remember me? Could he help me?

'Julius, it's Heather. Heather Lucas. I came to see you. I need to talk to you.'

He stood aside and I walked cautiously in to his house. The door shut almost silently behind me. I turned my head and looked at him, he looked at me.

'I am glad to see you again, Heather,' he said, speaking his strange guttural English. His voice sent a chill down my spine. There was something about the tone, the ice-hard stare of his eyes that made me want to draw away from him. I kept remembering how I'd seen him with Andrew's wrist in his hand, and Andrew's blood on his lips.

It was him. He'd started all this chaos. He was the one who lured innocent victims to his house, like a spider enticing flies into its web. But now he was the only one who could help me.

169

'I came to ask you . . . to ask you . . .' My voice faded and died.

Above us, in the room to the left at the top of the stairs, I could hear noises. Recognisable noises.

'I see that Andrew made you one of us.'

'One of us?'

'A vampire.'

'How can you tell?'

He smiled. A strange secret horrible smile. 'The way you look. The way you sound. I can always tell . . . to me it is as obvious as your colour.'

So he could tell I wasn't human any more. I wondered how, then with a start I realised what I'd just thought.

Human . . . Wasn't I human still . . . ?

'I'm *not* like you, Julius . . .'

'Oh, but you are. You are one of the undead. Like me. Like Andrew.'

I shook my head, but smiled to take the sting out of my words. 'I only drink animal blood. I don't kill people. I'm not like you or Andrew.'

'But you will be. It could be tomorrow, the day after, next year, the next century. You *will* kill. And once you have tasted human blood you will never ever turn back.'

Long moments passed as I studied him. 'That's why I came here. To get your help. Can we go upstairs to your room?'

'Of course.' Julius ushered me upstairs, following behind me. What was I doing? Getting in deeper and deeper. My heart was about to burst out of my chest. I forced myself to breathe slowly to try and slow down my heartbeat. Julius was no fool. He'd notice something if I wasn't very, very careful. At the top of the stairs, I forced myself not to look at the other door. The sounds continued, louder and more frantic than before.

Once in Julius' room, I couldn't suppress the shudder

of revulsion that ran through me. This was where it had all started.

Julius' small double bed was pushed against the wall. It hadn't been in the room during the party. The room was spartan to the point of being almost empty. Just the bed and a built-in wardrobe, and a bookcase crammed full of books. Shutters had been placed over the window in the room and nailed down. I hadn't noticed that before.

'Is that safe?' I pointed to the window as I turned back to Julius.

'Very. The shutters outside the window have also been nailed shut and the window has been painted black and covered.'

'You aren't taking any chances, are you?'

'I like it here. And I intend to stay a while.'

We watched each other. Looking at Julius, the little hope with which I had travelled withered slowly inside me.

'How long . . . how long have you been a vampire?' I asked.

'Seventeen years, four months, fourteen days.'

I stared at him, shocked. Whatever I'd been expecting, it wasn't that.

'So really you're what . . . Almost forty?'

Julius grinned. The grin of a twenty-year-old boy.

'Age to people like us is just a number. It means nothing.'

I hadn't realised.

'So I see. I bet . . . I bet you know more about what we are and what we can achieve than I've even yet imagined.'

'You will learn.'

Silence.

'Will you teach me?' I asked quietly.

171

His grin faded. It took all my courage not to look away as he scrutinised me.

'What about you and Andrew?' he asked at last.

'What about us?'

'What happened to all that angst and passion?'

I hated his sneering words, his mocking tone. Yet there was something else underlying them. Something I couldn't quite put my finger on. Sadness? Sorrow? It couldn't be, and yet . . .

'Where is the undying love you told me you both felt for each other?'

'Those two people don't exist any more, except as memories. They died that night in this room,' I replied slowly. 'It's taken me until this moment to realise it, that's all.'

'The love you had for each other is the reason you and Andrew are still alive,' he said harshly.

'Alive!' I breathed the word. Not living, just alive.

I'd taken on something I thought I could handle, something I thought I could control. Only instead of me taking control, it had. Like a fool, I'd really *believed* I could do this and win. I looked at the nailed-down shutters again. An inner sense told me the sunrise was approaching.

But not fast enough.

'Do you mind if I sit down?'

Julius shook his head. I sat on his bed and he came and sat beside me. My heartbeat was speeding up again, I almost couldn't hear the sounds coming from the room across the landing – almost.

'The sun will be up soon.' I looked straight ahead, too nervous to look at Julius.

'Where will you stay?'

'I was hoping you'd let me stay here for the day.' I licked my dry lips.

'My pleasure.'

172

He placed his hand under my chin and turned my head. Then he kissed me. I wanted to chuck up. I wanted to push him away and drag the back of my hand across my mouth to clean it. I did neither. I didn't kiss him back – but I didn't push him away either.

Time. I needed more time. And a plan. *Think of something, Heather.*

Julius drew away from me. He watched me silently.

'I'm looking for a bed for the day, not a love affair.' I forced myself to smile.

'You love Andrew still?'

'I told you, Andrew and Heather are dead.'

'And you blame me?'

Silence.

'I don't blame anyone. It's just one of those things. Julius . . . are there many others like us?'

'It depends on what you call "many".'

'How many of us have you . . . made?'

Julius considered. 'Andrew was the . . . third.'

'I'll tell him. Three is his lucky number.' I smiled.

Julius moved closer. I didn't move.

'So why are you here? You still haven't told me.'

'Yes I have. I want you to teach me everything you know. I can't wait years to get it right.'

'I do not have it right,' Julius laughed harshly. 'I still get things wrong. Like you and Andrew.'

'You still know more than me.' I shrugged. 'Tell me, how many times have you . . . drunk from real people? How many people have you . . . you . . .' I couldn't bring myself to say the rest.

'I feed about once a week. More in the summer when the tourists arrive.' He laughed.

'Is that why you have the parties? To invite strangers?'

'Why else?'

'I see. Your brother, is he a vampire too?'

173

'Marcus? Of course not! He stays away from this place. He loathes me.'

Marcus . . . Where had I heard that name before? I glanced over to the window shutters again.

'Why do you keep looking over there? That's the third time in the last ten minutes.'

So he *had* noticed.

'The sun will be up very soon.'

'That's the second time you've said that.'

I looked at him steadily. He didn't miss much. I mustn't make the mistake of underestimating him.

'I'm worried.'

'About what?'

'About this house. Is it safe? *Really* safe?'

'Of course. I told you. The windows . . .'

'Not just the windows,' I interrupted. 'The doors downstairs . . . are they safe?'

'There is only one door, the front door. And it has been – what is the word? – reinforced.'

'Yes, but is it safe?'

Julius frowned at me. 'What is the matter?'

I chewed on my bottom lip, nervously.

'Tell me,' he ordered.

'Andrew . . .' I bowed my head. 'Andrew is after me. I think he might have followed me here. I need somewhere safe to stay but I don't want to put you in danger . . .'

'From Andrew?' he laughed contemptuously. 'I do not fear Andrew.'

'I do. Your door downstairs doesn't look too solid. I think, to be on the safe side, I'd better go and look for something else.'

'You cannot go now.' He frowned at me. 'The sun will rise in only a few minutes.'

'I'm not staying here unless I know there's no way Andrew can get to me.'

'Come! Quickly! I will prove it to you.' Julius took my hand and stood up, pulling me after him.

I let him lead me out of the room. I paused on the landing to look at the door of the other room. It was silent now.

'You and I will feed together tonight,' he said, looking from the door to me.

'If you don't mind sharing.' I nodded.

'Sharing . . .' Julius looked as if he were choking on the word. 'It has been a long time since I have shared anything with anyone.'

We looked at one another.

'Andrew is stupid. And his loss is my gain. I will protect you.'

I didn't reply.

'Quick. Before the sun appears,' Julius said urgently.

We went downstairs. The door was a solid, polished piece of wood. It didn't even have panels. On the inside were two bolts, one above head height, the other at foot level. The lock was a standard one, but good quality. He opened the door, looking warily up at the lightening sky.

'See! I spoke the truth.' Julius pointed to the gap between the door and its frame. I looked at the hinges. They seemed new and sturdy enough. The door was thick wood and solid all the way through. In the door itself, above and below each hinge, there were steel bolts which sat in holes in the frame when the door was shut.

'Andrew's strong now. Like you. This door won't shut him out.'

'Of course it will.' Julius was getting impatient. The sky was even lighter now. It frightened me too. Every hair on my body was prickling and alarm bells were ringing. I had to get inside. I couldn't let the sun find me.

'Look! Shut the door and I will try to open it.' Julius was getting angry. 'Will that satisfy you?'

'Yes.'

I went back inside. The moment the door was shut I slid the bolts home and set the lock.

'Okay, try it now,' I called out.

The door shuddered as Julius rushed at it. 'See! See! This door will not move. Andrew will not get in here. Let me in.'

'Try it again.'

'No!' He was shouting now. 'Heather, let me in.'

'No. Try again.'

Julius pushed and kicked at the door again. 'Heather, the sun is almost above the horizon. *Let me in.*'

I backed away from the door.

'Heather . . . HEATHER. . . .'

'I hope the sun fries your ass, you bastard!' I screamed at him. 'This is for destroying my life. This is for destroying the lives of all your victims. YOU BASTARD!'

'HEATHER . . . LET ME IN . . . I BEG YOU . . .'

'No. Never.' I wiped my hand over my lips, eliminating all traces of that foul kiss he'd given me.

'Heather, the sun . . . The sun . . .'

'Did you really think I'd let you touch me? Did you really think I'd want you, after what Andrew and I had together? *What you took away from us?!*'

Julius laughed. Just that. He started laughing. And the sound froze my soul.

'See you in hell, Heather. See you . . . in . . . hell . . .'

His voice faded to nothing. I couldn't wait any longer. I scrambled up the stairs. The noise from the other room had started again, but I couldn't stop. I ran in to Julius' room, slammed the door behind me and fell on to his bed, exhausted.

The sun had come up.

Thirty

I awoke that evening with a pounding head and a heavy heart. The memory of what had happened – of what I'd done – came flooding back. I sat up slowly, then buried my head in my hands.

'You had no choice.' I kept saying, over and over. It didn't help. I told myself all sorts of things. Julius was a merciless killer – but he'd spared Andrew and me. Julius would have killed again if I hadn't stopped him – but he was capable of compassion. Julius was me in twenty years or two hundred years time – *maybe*. It was perhaps just a matter of time. And what then? Would someone put me out of my misery too? Julius . . . *My problem . . . Not my problem . . . My problem . . .*

Something I'd said that night weeks ago, had got to him. And now because of me . . . But I'd had no choice. No choice at all. *None.*

Wearily I stood up. I needed desperately to feed and even more desperately wished I didn't have to. Pain, like a concrete lump, sat in my chest. I longed to go back, back to before our holiday. Back to peace.

I tumbled out of the room and on to the landing. The door to the other room was locked, but the key was in the lock. I turned it and pulled open the door. A girl and a boy, both about my age or slightly older, threw themselves out of the room. If I hadn't been so weak from hunger, I would have seen them coming from a kilometre away. As it was, I only just managed to step out of the way.

'I'm not your enemy,' I said quickly. 'I'm not.'

The boy straightened up, pushing the girl behind him. I smiled at the gesture, then at them. The boy had light brown hair and light brown, scared eyes. He wore jeans and a sweatshirt, as did the girl. Her hair was darker, her eyes grey. They both had the same terrified expression on their faces. I recognised it at once. Just as I'd recognised their cries and pleas for help the previous night when I'd entered Julius' house. He'd ruined my life. I couldn't let Julius get anyone else. I couldn't let him do it to anyone else.

'Are you all right? He didn't hurt you?' I glanced down at their wrists. No marks. I was hungry. So hungry.

'You let us go?' the boy asked.

'Of course. Go on! Go!'

'Before he returns?'

I nodded. I was starving. 'Before he returns. Go to the police.'

Without another word they ran down the stairs and out the door. I followed. I had to feed before I passed out. Once outside, I looked up at the dark sky. It was going to rain. What was I thinking? The rain had started already, I just hadn't noticed until too late.

Coming back to London after almost a fortnight was a mistake, I knew, but it was the closest I'd been to happiness since I'd travelled out to see Julius. There were so many things to do and so little time to do them in. After seeing Mum and Jessica, the first thing I would do was find Andrew. We had to establish a truce. I had to persuade him that we were dangerous. Too dangerous. Would he see things my way? *He must* . . .

But what if he didn't? I asked myself. What then?

So many things had gone wrong already, but this wouldn't. We didn't have to be together, I knew it was too late for that, but Andrew must see that we should go somewhere where we wouldn't be a threat to those around us. Being with Julius for that short period had cleared my head on a number of things. It was time to face the truth. I couldn't let Andrew turn into another Julius. For the sake of what we'd once had . . . for the sake of what we'd once been.

But I was scared, no! . . . terrified! I could admit that without feeling like a coward. Andrew *must* understand. Julius was a warning, a live warning, of how much further there was to fall. It was time to take control. We both needed to say 'this far and no further'. And I'd make Andrew understand. I couldn't fail.

But first – to see my friends and, most importantly, my mum and my sister. I wanted desperately to see them all again.

One last time.

I walked down the street towards the Burger Bar gazing at every house, every shop, and grinning inanely. In spite of all that had happened here, it still felt like home. I stood and closed my eyes, breathing deeply. Carbon monoxide and pollution, but the air had never smelt sweeter. I could even smell the Burger Bar's greasy chips from half-way up the street. I couldn't wait to see the look on Diane's face when I saw her again, or the look on all my friends' faces.

Not that I'd stay very long. I wanted to spend most of tonight with Mum . . . I *wanted* to spend the whole night talking to her! I needed to tell someone the truth. Someone who still cared about me. It was dangerous, I knew, but I couldn't let that stop me. I sighed and opened my eyes, and was just about to start walking again when I saw him. Morgan.

And he saw me. He was at one end of the street and I was at the other. Neither of us moved.

'So you're back,' I heard him mutter to himself.

I realised I was holding my breath, and let it out with

a hiss. Morgan was standing under a street lamp so his face was illuminated. I tried to focus on his eyes. They still held the human spark that mine now lacked.

So Andrew hadn't made him one of us. Morgan smiled secretly and turned around to walk back the way he'd come. I let him go. I wanted nothing to do with him, just with his brother.

I took a few more steps towards the Burger Bar but it was as if a light inside of me had dimmed. Seeing Morgan again had shifted my previous decisions. What had seemed so clear and obvious before, now seemed hasty. Maybe I shouldn't see my friends again, it might be too painful. Better to leave things the way they were. Maybe I should just go to see Mum and Jessica, then seek out Andrew.

I turned around and went home via the park. I jumped over the railing and sat on the swings in the children's playground, kicking myself slowly backwards and forwards for a few minutes. It'd be the last time I did that, too.

Time to figure out exactly what to say to Mum. Nothing came into my head. Over the last week, all I'd thought about was Andrew and what we'd say to each other. I'd tried to imagine all the scenarios, like planning chess moves in my head. (I was useless at chess.) My dreams of what it could be like fought with the likely reality . . . and snippets of the conversations I'd had with Andrew in my night dreams came back to haunt me.

'*I want to wake up and find this has all been a dream. The worse dream of my life. I want to wake up to find that there are no such things as vampires, except in feature films and fiction books. I want life back.*'

'*Every time I go to sleep, I hope for the same thing,*' Andrew says sadly. '*I think to myself, when I wake up it'll be day. But it never is. It's always night.*'

'I miss daylight. The sun, blue skies, white clouds . . .'
'I miss . . . feelings.' Andrew moves towards me. 'I miss being really happy or really sad. I don't feel anything any more, except for you, only you.'
'Hatred?'
Andrew shakes his head. 'I don't hate you.'
He smiles at me. I smile back, sadly.
'Our capacity to sympathise, to empathise – is dying. And it'll get worse, won't it? There'll come a time when no one or nothing will matter. Killing others won't matter because we can't die. Life won't matter because we can live forever. It's started already, hasn't it?'
Andrew holds me. I hug him back. I'll never let him go again.
'I'm sorry, Heather.'
'I'm sorry, Andrew.'
We walk off into the sunrise together.
With a sigh, I opened my eyes. A dream. That's all it was. A fantasy. I got up and set off for home.
'Reality stinks,' I hissed to myself. Reality was a nightmare.
Within three streets of Mum's house, I heard screaming.
'Jessica! Oh my God! Jessica's still in there!' The fear and panic in Mum's voice set me running immediately. I was there within seconds. And what I saw brought me to an abrupt halt.
Our house was on fire.
Hungry orange and yellow flames belched out of the bedrooms at the front of the house. I could feel the intense heat even from where I was standing.
'Mum . . . MUM!' I shouted as I ran towards it.
Mum turned her head as she heard me call. She looked as though she'd aged ten years since I'd last seen her. Her eyes were huge, wild, her shoulders drooped forward. Her neck muscles were taut.

'Mum . . .' I whispered as I drew near to her.

'Heather, Jessica's in there. I couldn't get her out. She's still in her room . . .'

Mrs Tout came and put her arms around Mum's shoulders. Mrs Tout was crying too. Quite a crowd had gathered by now. There was panic and pandemonium as one of our neighbours tried to get near the house but was beaten back by the flames. There were cries for the fire brigade, and the police, and an ambulance.

'I'll get her out,' I said to mum.

I raced towards the house.

'Heather, no!'

Ignoring her, I battered on the door with my fists. It gave way immediately. The heat was intense and choking black smoke rushed to meet me, but I could just about bear it. For the very first time I was profoundly grateful for what I now was, for the strength it gave me.

'I'm coming, Jessica.'

I dashed up the stairs, coughing until my lungs stung and my eyes wept. Flames ate at the banisters and snatched at my jacket, setting it alight. I pulled it off as I ran and flung it behind me.

At the top of the house, the fire had taken control of the front two bedrooms and was creeping towards Jessica's bedroom. Smoke was everywhere. I ran straight to the room and kicked the door in. The smoke had reached there and it hung in the air, slowly curling downwards. Through the haze I could see my sister huddled under the window at the other side of the room. Her breathing was laboured, heavy. Running over to her, I picked her up. She lay limp like a puppet with its strings cut.

'Jessica . . .' I cradled her against me. 'Oh Jessica. Hang on, I'll get you out of here.'

I tried to go back the way I'd come but the flames

were whipping around outside the door. I could stand the flames for long enough to run through them, but there was no way that Jessica could.

Think, Heather! I tried to calm my mounting panic. Should I try to make it to the bathroom? I could douse Jessica in water once there to protect her from the flames until I could make it out of the house. But I still had to get through the raging fire outside her room first. And that I couldn't risk. I heard an ominous series of cracks, followed by the sound of falling and it took only a few seconds to realise that the top of the staircase was collapsing. I looked around the room. There had to be *something* I could do.

I put Jessica over my shoulder, her face against my back, and pushed against the window with one hand. It was shut fast with paint. There were specks of blood on the upper frame. Jessica had tried to open the window too, damaging her hands in the process. Angrily, I pushed harder. I thought I would have to put my fist through the glass, but I didn't have to. The window flew open.

I climbed out on to the window ledge. Taking a deep breath, I threw myself into the air to land on my two feet seconds later in the garden. I turned Jessica around to check on her immediately. Her warm breath fanned my cheek. I could hear her heart beating, slow but steady. I smiled. Holding her tightly, I jumped over the fence into Mrs Tout's garden. I walked down the path to the side gate. Three steps, and my knees almost buckled under me. Suddenly weary to the point of exhaustion, I forced myself to keep walking. Opening the gate, I walked out of the front garden and on to the street. I saw Mum – still staring frantically at our house. I tried walking towards her, but my knees gave out from under me. I tried to call, but my throat felt as if I'd swallowed a bucket of sand.

All I wanted to do was cry.

'There she is!' someone in the crowd shouted.

Mrs Tout turned her head, then pointed. Mum followed the direction of her finger ... I tried to smile. Mum dashed across the road towards me and I looked past her at all the people watching our house burn.

Morgan and Andrew were standing together, watching. And then I knew why our house was on fire. I struggled to my feet, an action which took all the energy I had left. It was as if everyone else in the world had disappeared ... There was no sight, no sound, nothing but Morgan and Andrew.

And I hated them.

I hated them, with every breath that I took and every cell in my body. Morgan for his hatred and his insults and his narrow mind and his stupidity, but most of all I hated Andrew. 'My' Andrew. A blood drinker. A vampire. A murderer. *A liar!* He'd wanted me to share in all he was and all he could be, and he'd succeeded. I loathed him.

'Heather, are you all right? Is Jessica all right?' Mum appeared, blocking my view. She was laughing and crying all at once, hugging the two of us to her, as if she'd never let us go. Jessica began to cough fitfully, her eyes still closed. In the distance I heard the wail of approaching sirens.

'We're fine, Mum,' I whispered. I looked over her shoulder, but Andrew and Morgan had gone.

'Just fine.'

I thought, okay Andrew you win. If it's a war you want, then it's a war you've got.

Thirty-One

'Heather, your ears are stuck in your backside!' Mum stormed.

'Mum, I'm not going to stay overnight at the hospital, taking up a bed. I feel fine,' I argued for the umpteenth time.

'I still don't know how you did it.' Mrs Tout shook her head as she brought in yet another pot of peppermint tea.

It was after midnight now. The fire brigade had put out the fire and most of the upstairs of our house was gutted. They and the police were still shifting through the debris to find out what had caused the fire.

An ambulance had taken us all to Lewisham Hospital. Jessica was fine, but they'd decided to keep her in overnight for observation. I had superficial burns to my hands and arms and the casualty doctors had suggested keeping me in too but I wouldn't let them. How could I? I needed desperately to feed. And besides, how could I explain that already, under my bandages, my skin was knitting together, healing. It was a peculiar sensation, like being pricked by many blunt needles. And once I'd fed again, my skin would heal faster still. Then there was the little matter of hiding from the daylight in a hospital ward . . .

'I only popped out for a second to borrow some sugar for a cup of coffee. If anything had happened to either of you . . .' Mum shuddered.

'But it didn't,' Mrs Tout said firmly. 'So don't go brooding over what never happened.'

I smiled at her. She was in her element now that she had someone to look after. I glanced across at the television. On it sat a plethora of photographs of her husband who had died some years ago. I thought of all the photos Mum kept of Dad. I remembered the time just after he'd died. Mum hadn't said much, but I heard her crying, night after night. Dad had died of cancer.

I remembered too, how, just after his funeral — when she'd thought she was alone — Mum had taken off her wedding ring and thrown it at the living-room wall, silent tears streaming down her face.

It's strange the things that stick in the mind. Like, if I lived to be four thousand, I'd never forget tonight, and seeing Morgan and Andrew watching me.

'Are you sure you're all right, Heather?' Mrs Tout asked.

I nodded.

'Now you can all stay with me until the insurance comes through so you can get your place renovated,' she said firmly.

'But we can stay in a hotel. I have the money,' Mum protested.

'Nonsense! Why throw good money away? I have plenty of room, and you know how much I'd enjoy the company.'

'I know.' Mum smiled.

We sipped at our tea. I was loathe to break the companionable silence but I had to.

'Mrs Tout, do you have a sheet of writing paper I can use?'

'Why d'you need paper?' Mum asked.

'To write a letter.'

'Can't it wait until the morning?' she frowned.

'I wish it could.'

'Of course, dear. It's in the kitchen. I'll just go and get it.' Mrs Tout bustled out of the room.

'What's the matter?' Mum asked me, quietly.

'You wouldn't believe me even if I did tell you.'

'You said that once before.'

'And I was right. You didn't believe me.'

Mum frowned at me. Then she gave me a puzzled smile. 'You always were a strange child, Heather. I could live to be one hundred and still not understand you.'

'I take after you then, don't I?' I teased.

Mum and I smiled together. It'd been a long time since we'd done that.

'I was worried about you,' she said, her smile fading. 'You went away for such a long time. You seemed to disappear into thin air.'

'Mum, I was only gone for two weeks and I did phone a few times.'

'It's not the same.'

'I guess not.' I sighed.

'And you're going away again, aren't you.' It wasn't a question.

'I have to, Mum.' I lowered my head.

'Are you going with Andrew?'

'Please don't ask any more questions. Just ... I wouldn't go if I didn't have to.' I looked up at her. 'You were right about a lot of things but please don't say "I told you so".' I couldn't help it, I started to cry.

Mum stared, her eyes wide.

'What's the matter? You've seen me cry before.'

She stood up and walked over to me. She placed a finger under my left eye. A single tear drop ran on to it.

A single tear drop of blood.

Thirty-Two

Andrew,
I'm sure you want to see me as badly as I want to
see you. I will be at the deserted office building on
the corner of Acre Road and Gulliver Street, tomor-
row night at eight-thirty. DON'T bring anyone else.
They'd only get hurt.
Heather.

I read and re-read what I'd written. It wasn't perfect,
but it would do. It would get him there.

Funny how nothing ever happened the way you
thought or hoped it would. Even when I came back
from Fipoli the second time, I'd still hoped that the
situation between Andrew and me could be salvaged
somehow. Now I knew that was impossible. I didn't
look for it and I didn't want it – but Andrew and I
were at war. A war between two people. And we had
one final battle to fight. A battle I wasn't about to lose.
Maybe I'd come home too late. Maybe I should never
have left. All I knew was that Andrew was evil. He was
dangerous and he'd never leave my family alone now.
Well, if he wanted me so badly, he could have me.

As for my letter, the question was: how to deliver it?
I couldn't risk another trip to his attic.

Hell! Why not just post it through the front door?
I'd had enough of jumping over this and climbing up
that for one night. And if Andrew were home, then
we'd resolve the situation that much sooner. I folded

the letter and put it in the matching envelope Mrs Tout had given me.

Fifteen minutes later, after a quick feed, I pushed the letter, addressed to Andrew, through the Harrison letter box. I turned around to walk back home. I'd only reached the gate when the front door opened. I didn't bother turning around.

'I knew you'd turn up.'

Reluctantly I stopped walking at the sound of Morgan's rasping voice.

'Then you weren't disappointed.'

I turned, my hands clasped behind my back. Morgan had the letter in his hands. Looking at him, I wondered how I'd ever let him get to me. He was nothing. Insignificant. An ignorant bigot, led on by his brother.

'Andrew's not here. You're welcome to come in and wait for him,' he suggested silkily.

'No, thank you.'

We regarded each other. The intense hatred on Morgan's face bounced right off me. His problem, not mine.

'Tell Andrew I called. And give him the letter.'

Without taking his eyes off me, Morgan tore open the envelope. With a sardonic smirk he lowered his gaze to read the letter out loud.

'That's fine with us,' he said when he'd finished reading. 'That's fine with *both* of us. But not the office building. Not somewhere that you've specified. How about right here?'

'In your house?'

'In our house.'

'What about your parents?'

Morgan's eyes narrowed. 'The house will be all ours. Mum and Dad have gone on a cruise while Mum recuperates.'

'Fine with me.'

'Tomorrow. Eight-thirty.'

I started walking.

'And Heather . . . ?'

'What?' I didn't look back.

'If you don't turn up then we'll come and get you. Understand?'

I turned around.

'Morgan, I don't want you,' I said quietly. 'But don't push your luck.'

I don't know whether it was my words or my tone that got to Morgan, but something did.

I carried on walking but the front door didn't slam shut until I was half-way down the street.

Thirty-Three

I awoke the moment the sun sank below the horizon. I'd slept in the one place I thought Andrew wouldn't try to find me, my own home. The previous night, when I was sure that I wasn't being followed, I'd gone back to what was now a charred and sopping-wet home and crept into the cellar. I thought it probable that Andrew would get Morgan to try and find me during the day. That way they could jump me, but I was determined to make sure they didn't succeed.

I'd meet with Andrew on my own terms.

They shouldn't have burnt out our house. They shouldn't have put Jessica in danger. My sister was still in hospital. The doctors wanted to keep her in for another night.

I had the rest of the night plotted out very carefully indeed. I knew what had to be done and where I had to be at every minute of every hour.

The first thing I did was pop next door to use Mrs Tout's shower. Mum was there. She put the toilet seat down and sat on it while we talked about nothing in particular. Odd, embarrassed silences littered our conversation. There was so much I wanted to say but couldn't. From the look on her face she was having the same problem.

'The police told me how the fire was started,' she said after another of the pauses.

'Oh yes?' I poked my head out from behind the shower curtain. 'How?'

'Someone threw a phosphorous-based incendiary

191

device through your bedroom window. The moment the bottle that it was in smashed, the phosphorous ignited and set fire to the carpet.'

'I see. I thought it had to be something like that,' I mumbled, returning behind the curtain.

'I'd like to know who would do such a thing. It was despicable!'

'Don't worry, Mum. They'll pay.'

She didn't reply.

I washed my hair and scrubbed myself until I tingled. After drying and moisturising my skin, I slipped on the new black shirt and black jeans that I'd asked Mum to buy for me during the day. At last I was ready.

'Where will you be sleeping tonight?' Mum asked as I headed downstairs.

'I'm not sure.'

I opened the front door.

'Heather, you know who did it, don't you?'

'Did what?'

'You know who set fire to our house.'

I didn't answer.

'Heather . . . don't go after them.' Her hand was at my shoulder. 'Tell the police. Don't go after them yourself.'

'I . . . I don't know what you're talking about,' I said lightly.

'Oh, Heather, don't go seeking revenge. Revenge has a habit of rebounding.'

'I'll remember that.' I smiled. 'See you Mum. Say hello to Jessica for me. Tell her she's a scabby oik . . . Tell her I love her.'

Mum looked at me. 'I'll see you tomorrow, dear,' she said sadly.

'Mum . . . I love you.' I spoke quietly.

I didn't wait to see her face or hear her reply. I

stepped out on to the front path, closing the door firmly behind me.

'I love you too, Heather,' she whispered.

I bowed my head. I wanted to go back into the house and never come out, but I didn't. Instead I walked through the gate, forcing myself not to look back. I headed for the station and the train to take me in to town. I had things to buy and prepare before I could do anything else. Then I'd go and see Diane. I needed her help too. One way or another, tonight would see the resolution of the mess I'd made of my life.

Thirty-Four

'Hi, Morgan. Is Andrew home?'

'He's busy at the moment,' Morgan replied tersely. 'It's . . . it's Diane, isn't it?'

'That's right. Tell Andrew I'm here please. It's really important.'

'Who is it, Morgan?' Andrew came down the stairs.

'Hi, Andrew. It's me.' Diane smiled. 'Can I speak to you in private?'

'Can't it wait?' Andrew asked impatiently.

Diane shook her head.

'Oh, all right. I'll see you inside, Morgan.' Andrew took his brother's place at the door.

'What is it, Diane?' Andrew asked warily.

From my position on the roof of the house three doors down from Andrew's home, I could hear everything but I could see only Diane. I didn't want to risk getting any closer in case Andrew heard me.

'I've got a message from Heather,' Diane began slowly.

Get it right Diane, I prayed silently.

I'd had a real job getting her to help me in the first place, especially since I'd refused to tell her what was going on. That was for her own protection . . . the less she knew, the better. How could I tell her what I was now? What Andrew was? I'd explained some of it to Mum, an explanation she hadn't believed either until she'd seen my reflection and my tears . . . I couldn't bear to go through it all a second time.

Finally, reluctantly, Diane had stopped asking me to

tell her what was happening and agreed to help me. But it took a lot of persuasion.

Now Diane said to Andrew, 'Heather wants to meet you at the original rendezvous – she said you'd know where that is. She wants to talk to you. Just you, and just talk. She wants to call a truce.'

Silence.

'And if I say no?' Andrew asked at last.

'You'll have to take that up with her,' Diane shrugged. 'I'm just delivering the message. Are you two having some sort of trouble?'

I would have laughed except I was annoyed with her. I hadn't told her to add that question.

'Just a minute. I'll get my jacket,' Andrew said after another pause.

I didn't even dare to breathe a sigh of relief. He went back in to the house. Diane walked down the path to the gate.

'Morgan, I'm going out. I'll be back soon,' Andrew yelled.

Morgan emerged from wherever to stand in the hall. 'You can't go out now. What if Heather turns up here?' he whispered. The anger in his voice couldn't hide the fear.

'She won't. She wants me to meet her in the office building she talked about in her letter,' Andrew replied softly.

'You're not really going are you? It might be a trap.'

'I'll take that chance.'

'And if she *does* come here?'

'Why should she? It's me she wants. I just want all this to be over.'

'You didn't see the way she looked at me yesterday.'

'Relax, Morgan. I promise you, Heather wants only me.'

'You two are being very mysterious. What's going on?' Diane called from the gate.

No one answered. Morgan and Andrew walked out the door, on to the garden path.

'I wish someone would tell me what's going on?' Diane complained. 'Heather didn't explain and you two aren't saying much. Honestly!'

'Andrew, let me come with you,' Morgan whispered insistently.

'No,' Andrew shook his head. 'I didn't want you to stay in the house anyway. This is between Heather and me.'

'I have to look out for you. You're my brother.'

'Thanks, but I'll be fine,' Andrew smiled. 'I'll see you later.'

'If anything happens to you . . .'

'It won't.'

'If anything does, I'll find her. If it takes the rest of my life, I'll find her,' Morgan said, but for his brother's ears only.

'You fuss too much,' Andrew pushed at his brother's shoulder. 'You're turning into Mum,' he teased.

Morgan made a face but didn't say anything.

'I'll see you,' Andrew said.

Morgan went back into his house, closing the front door behind him.

Thirty-Five

Andrew and Diane walked out on to the street. They turned right, away from me.

'Shall I come?' Diane asked.

'To where?' Andrew asked lightly.

'To wherever it is that you're going.'

'Diane, you are the *nosiest*! This is between Heather and me.'

'She's my friend too,' Diane said stubbornly. 'And there's something going on here ...'

'Diane, go home. I'll see you tomorrow night.'

'Oh, all right then,' she said reluctantly. 'If you need me, you know where I live.'

'Yeah! In the Burger Bar.'

'Got it in one!' Diane laughed.

I watched them walk down the street, waiting for them to turn the corner. Then I ran and jumped until I was on the Harrison's roof. I tiptoed down the sloping roof towards the back of the house, swinging myself down to the window-ledge of the back bedroom which Mrs Harrison used as her sewing-room. I tried the window but it was locked.

So what now? I wasn't going to let a locked window stop me. I could easily crash through it but I wanted to keep the element of surprise on my side. I shifted my position slightly and studied the window. With each movement, the weapon slung across my back rocked into me. I tried re-adjusting its position but it made little difference. Pursing my lips, I forced myself to focus on the first task before me, opening the window.

Holding on to the guttering with one hand, I tried to push slowly against the glass. It creaked ominously. I clenched my fists with frustration, my fingernails digging into my palms. Fingernails . . . it was worth a try.

Still using one hand to hold on to the guttering, I used the fingernail of the index finger of my other hand to draw around the window lever. It made a definite impression, like a glass cutter. I worked around my semi-circle again and then a third time. It was just about ready to drop out now. I took a deep breath. The next bit would take fast work. I pushed at the glass, and as it gave way I dropped my hand under it to catch it.

It worked.

And I hadn't made any noise. I slipped my hand through the hole in the glass and opened the window, then stepped inside.

Now to find Morgan.

Morgan was in the kitchen, drinking beer from a bottle.

I stood still and watched him as he drank, his back to me. Half-way through a gigantic swig, Morgan lowered the bottle suddenly. Every muscle in his body tensed. His head turned just ahead of the rest of his body. I thought the look on his face when he realised that he was alone in the house with me would bring me something. Satisfaction. Gratification. But I felt nothing.

'Hello, Morgan,' I said quietly.

'Andrew isn't here.' Morgan's voice was sharp.

'I'm here to . . . *see* . . . you . . . ' I smiled.

Morgan's lips thinned, his face grew pale.

When would I start to enjoy this?

He made a sudden break for the cutlery drawer. I didn't move.

'Do you know how ridiculous you look?' I said as he brought out a carving knife.

Morgan sprang, obviously deciding that attack was

the best form of defence. He swung the knife. To my eyes he was moving in slow motion. I saw the knife coming with no trouble at all. I grabbed his wrist and squeezed. He howled in agony and dropped the knife. It clattered on to the floor.

'Run . . .' I commanded. 'RUN!'

And, like the coward he was, he did. Had our roles been reversed, I would never have given him that satisfaction. I listened. He was at the front door trying to open it. I waited until I heard it open, before I moved. I was there in a second. Morgan wasn't aware of my presence until I shoved the front door shut before he had it even half-way open.

'Oh no you don't,' I told him. 'You didn't open the front door when you tried to burn my mum alive in her house.'

Morgan shrank against the wall behind him. 'We . . . We w-waited until she went out . . . to a n-neighbour's house . . .' Morgan's voice was uneven now, and panic-stricken.

'So you *were* involved. I wasn't sure. Thanks for letting me know.'

Morgan stared, realising what he'd just revealed.

'So it was my sister you wanted to kill?'

'No! Andrew was furious. He wasn't l-listening properly. He w-wanted you. We didn't know your sister as in the h-house. I swear. It was a mistake. We thought . . .'

'Don't think, Morgan. It only gets you into trouble.'

'Heather . . .'

'Run.'

He looked at me, his eyes pleading, as his mouth could or would not.

'Run . . .' I whispered.

I stretched out my hand towards him. He took off up the stairs. This game I was playing revolted me. All

199

at once I just wanted to end it. I climbed wearily up the stairs after Morgan.

'ANDREW!' Morgan screamed.

He ran into his bedroom, locking the door behind him. One push from me brought the door completely off its hinges.

Morgan and I stood there watching each other.

'Your mother was an accident. But you won't be.'

'Please . . .' he pleaded.

'Shush!' I put my finger over my lips as I walked towards him.

I pinned him against the wall, my hand against his chest. With my other hand I lifted Morgan's wrist to my mouth, looking straight into his terror-filled eyes.

But I couldn't do it.

Go on, Heather. He deserves it. This is your chance for revenge, a voice inside me said.

I didn't blink as I watched him.

Go on, Heather . . .

I played the whole scene over in my head, just as I'd imagined it, over and over.

I bite. And drink, feeling Morgan's heartbeat grow faster and faster and more and more frantic under my hand. He struggles but it's useless.

And still I drink.

Until at last I am the only thing keeping Morgan on his feet. I release him. He slips slowly down the wall and on to the floor. His blood, still warm upon my lips, trickles down my chin. Licking wet lips, I relish the sweet, metallic taste. It burns through me, warming my stomach. Liquid fire, burning its way through my entire body like cheap tonic wine.

I pull Morgan to his feet, his head drooping like a dying flower. His heartbeat is almost one continuous throb, now, as his heart tries frantically to pump his remaining blood around his body. I pull him to me, my

200

mouth seeking a particular part of his neck. I bite hard, then again, deeper. But not to drink. I am sated. I let go of him. Immediately, he falls to the floor, blood gushing from his neck . . .

A wonderful dream. But that was all it was.

'You're lucky, Morgan. You'll never know quite how lucky.' I released his wrist and took my hand away from over his racing heart. 'I want to hurt you. I want to hurt you so much. Like you've hurt me and mine. You're scum, Morgan. But if I kill you, I'm no better than you and Andrew. And I *am* better.'

Morgan's eyes were still wild, fearful. I doubted if he even knew what I was saying.

'But I owe you this.' I slapped him, not as hard as I could, but hard enough. He went out like a candle flame in a gust of wind. But he was alive.

Then I heard it. There . . . I raised my head and listened. A noise, sharp and grating, came from downstairs. Wood against wood. A window being carefully, cautiously opened.

Andrew.

He was doing his best not to make a sound but I heard him anyway. Did he really think I wouldn't? Or did he think I'd be too busy with his brother to notice anything else. So he'd heard his brother's cry for help . . . not that that mattered now.

I stopped breathing and turned my head to listen. I heard the slight scrape of a shoe heel against the wood of the window-sill.

He'd come for me.

The window fell shut, the sound echoing throughout the house. I heard Andrew's soft curse.

I thought, at last it will all be over.

Andrew and I will meet, and only one of us will survive.

Thirty-Six

My fingers shaking, I unhooked the loaded crossbow resting against my back. Once again, I checked to ensure that the safety-catch was on. It was a small crossbow, only about thirty-two or thirty-three centimetres in length. Its handle was fashioned in the same manner as the handle of a gun. I tried to remember the proper name for a gun handle. The stock? But what did I know? I loathed weapons.

The woman in the camping shop had been very enthusiastic when she showed me how it worked.

'It's the very latest model, you know. Safety-catch, a trigger mechanism, a two-stage sight which you can set yourself ...' She had come out from behind the counter to show me how it all worked.

At first I'd watched her talking rather than the crossbow. The two men serving behind the counter wore jeans and T-shirts. She wore an army combat jacket, khaki trousers and Timberland boots. I'd wondered if she thought that was the only way prospective customers would take her seriously.

Then I'd turned my attention to the crossbow. It took me a good five minutes before I could summon up the courage to hold the thing. It was lighter in weight than I thought it would be. Lighter and colder.

'It also comes with six bolts in their own case,' the shop assistant continued. 'Can I ask what it's for?'

'It's a present.'

'I'm sure the man you give this to is going to love it,' she smiled.

'I hope it'll be a surprise.'

'It comes in its own box, so if you wrap it, he won't be able to guess what it is. I'm sure he'll love it.'

I looked at her but didn't answer. I found myself annoyed that she should assume the bow was for a man, but then I shrugged and told myself that really it was a compliment. Women had more sense than to be impressed by such dangerous toys.

So what was I doing buying it? And even if I bought it, could I really *use* it?

I'd left, clutching the carrier bag which held my purchase to my chest. Walking quickly away from the shop, I was stopped by two animal rights campaigners.

'Excuse me, will you sign our petition?'

'What's it about?'

'We want to stop cruelty to animals...'

'And encourage people to think about eating alternatives to meat...' said another.

I signed.

So here I was, staring at the crossbow in my hand and once again wondering if I could use the thing. Could I actually look Andrew in the eye and pull the trigger? Would it come to that? I looked down at Morgan.

Don't think about it, I told myself. Don't think about anything, except surviving.

I double-checked the bolt which sat in the groove of the crossbow barrel. It wasn't one of the metal bolts which had come with the crossbow. This was a long, thin stake I'd carved myself from hard, hard wood. A stake with a sharp, sharp point. I almost smiled.

The stake was held firmly in place by the metal pressure catch above it. I knew it would fire all right. The question was, would it do the job? No, not *the* question, just one of them.

Don't think about it...

203

I crept out on to the landing, then paused listening for Andrew.

'Heather? Heather, I know you're up there.'

I gripped the crossbow tighter in my right hand and walked towards the top of the stairs, my right hand hidden behind my back. Andrew stood in the hall, looking up at me. The sight of him sent an unexpected and unwelcome jolt through my body. Before me was the image of the person I'd fallen in love with. The image of the man I'd wanted to share my body with. A million years ago.

'Where's Morgan?' he asked quietly.

'Lying down in his room.'

Pause.

'What did you do to him?'

'The same thing both of you tried to do to my family.'

'What if I tell you that I didn't have anything to do with the fire at your house? I never...'

'Don't tell me you never! You're the one doing the Chemistry A Level. Who else made that phosphorous bomb? Morgan? Your brother couldn't make up his own mind, much less make up a bomb. I've thought this through until my head is spinning. I still don't want to believe you'd do that to my family and our house, but I know it was you. Your brother just admitted as much. Don't lie to me, Andrew, not any more.'

'It was a mistake,' he said at last.

'Funny. That's what your brother said,' I replied bitterly. 'What was the point of your little present through my window? To get me here? No...it wasn't even that, was it? You just wanted to get me.'

He didn't answer. He didn't have to.

'Why?' I whispered.

'For the same reason you're hiding whatever it is you've got in your right hand.' His voice was harsh. His eyes were giving me frost-bite.

204

'It's not the same at all. Why do you hate me so much for being the same as you?'

'But you're not. Don't you see? And you won't change,' he shouted at me. 'It should all be perfect, but you want to hold on to what we were. You want to drag me back down to nothing.'

'Andrew, you don't get it, do you?' I shook my head sadly. 'What we have now is nothing. What we are now is nothing. Can't you see that?'

Silence.

So cold. When did it become so cold?

'Morgan's dead, isn't he?'

I didn't answer. Andrew's lips thinned. I watched them in isolation, then I looked at his cheeks, his hair, his eyes, his hands. He was angry. All he had to do was listen to know that Morgan was still alive. I could hear his brother's unconscious breathing. If Andrew wanted to, he could have heard it to, but I was the only thing on his mind now. He wouldn't allow anyone or anything else to enter his head.

'You fed on him.' It wasn't a question. Andrew started walking slowly up the stairs towards me.

'Tell me Pete is the one and only person you've killed,' I challenged. I dropped my right arm to my side. 'Tell me, you haven't killed any one else since I've been away and I'll give you my bow by the handle, right here, right now.'

Andrew halted on the fourth step. His eyes travelled from my face to the crossbow in my hand.

'Tell me. Go on.'

He didn't come any closer.

'That's what I thought.' I laughed harshly. 'You're evil, Andrew. It's what you've become. We both knew it wouldn't stop with Pete. Pete was just the first. No... I was the first.'

Andrew didn't deny it.

205

'Someone's got to stop you,' I whispered.

'You?'

'There is no one else. We both know that. And...
And that's why you're scared of me.'

I waited for Andrew to laugh in my face. He didn't.

'Well, we're both here, Andrew. What happens now?'

I don't know how long we stood watching one
another, moments or minutes.

*Say it doesn't matter. Say it's all a mistake. Invite me
to walk with you to greet the sunrise. Say it...say
it...*

Andrew vaulted over the banister, down into the hall.
In less than a second he was gone. I leaned over the
balustrade.

'Andrew...?'

Nothing.

What did it mean? Was Andrew going to leave me
alone? Had he heard his brother breathing and realised
I hadn't killed him. He must have done. Hope, long
extinguished, ignited within me.

'Is it over?' I breathed. 'Let it be over.'

Without warning, every light in the house went out.

Thirty-Seven

I gasped before I could stop it. Momentarily I froze, before sprinting for one of the bedrooms.

Andrew... He'd turned off the electricity. *Bastard!*

But I could see in the dark. I had night vision. Andrew knew that. So why switch off all the lights? To throw me off balance, I realised. And it had worked.

I should have stood my ground at the top of the stairs. I should never have run. Andrew knew me well. I'd been right about how it would end. I didn't want to be right, but I was.

I crouched low, forcing myself not to panic. At least I knew that he was still downstairs with the electricity fuse box. And I'd hear him when he came upstairs. No matter how quiet he tried to be, I'd hear him. I stopped breathing and listened harder. With a start, I realised I was in Andrew's room. Ironic.

Don't think about that. Think about surviving.

I looked around. I could see in the dark but I didn't want to rely solely upon my eyes. Bowing my head, I concentrated on using other senses. I closed my eyes, my grip on the crossbow slackening momentarily.

I don't want this. I DON'T WANT THIS. I tried to get the thought out of my head but it wouldn't budge.

Andrew, what happened to us?... Stop thinking like you're in a soap opera, Heather!

I leaned against the wall, my eyes still closed, the crossbow now a part of my right hand.

Two months ago, the world was normal. So was I. So was Andrew. The biggest things in my life had been passing my exams the following year and which university to attend, and making love for the first time. What would have happened if Andrew and I had made love, just once? Would it have made any difference? I'd never know now.

Now my life was...nothing. I'd done things I couldn't bear to think about, and it still wasn't all over.

An almost imperceptible creak on the landing had my eyes open instantly. He'd jumped up. I'd forgotten about the jumping. I crouched even further down, waiting.

Outside, Andrew gasped. I turned my head, to see through the wall, his location pinpointed. He'd found his brother. But knowing Morgan was alive wouldn't change Andrew's resolve. Strange, but at that moment I didn't hate Andrew any more. I wasn't scared of him any more. I was still scared, more than scared, but not of him. My hand and head turned to face the bedroom door. It was the only way in and I was ready.

Stand up or stay crouched – what should I do? I exhaled slowly, oh so slowly.

Stay crouched, I thought. Stay down and low. My eyes never left the entrance to Andrew's room. With my left hand, I gently fingered the other stake in my jacket pocket. If I missed, would I get a second chance? Doubtful.

Don't miss then. Come on, Andrew. Get it over. I just want this to be over.

I listened harder.

Where are you? Listening for me? It's not so easy coming after me, is it? I'm not the soft target my mum and sister were.

The hairs on my nape began prickling. Something was wrong. There was no...*presence* in the house. I felt alone. But I couldn't be. Andrew wouldn't go away and leave me, not after finding his brother. *Would he?*

208

Carefully, I began to rise, my eyes never leaving the bedroom door.

The smash of wood, the shattering of glass had my head whipping around.

The window...

Screaming, I raised my arm and fired wildly towards the window. The stake flew like a bullet, straight out of the shattered window. I fled around the door and out of the room, one hand still holding my crossbow, the other trying frantically to find my jacket pocket containing the other stake.

Down the stairs, Heather. Get downstairs.

The stake was in my left hand.

Down the stairs...

My legs disappeared from under me. I fell forward, landing heavily. Andrew grabbed my legs. The stake flew out of my hand and down the stairs, my head and upper body flopping forward over the top steps.

'No!'

I kicked and lashed out, against Andrew dragging me backwards. Cold fear, untamed and uncontrollable, gave me a strength I'd never had before. I kicked out, harder, my foot walloping him on the side of his face. I threw myself down the stairs after the stake.

'HEATHER...'

He was shouting at me. I couldn't hear. I didn't listen. The blood rushing through my body drowned out all other sounds. Like the fear I could smell, salty and sour, overwhelming all other smells. I stretched out my fingers.

Right there. The stake was right there, teasing my fingernails. Andrew was still shouting. I didn't want to hear.

Please don't make me hear. I can't bear it.

Got it! The stake was in my hand now. I pulled the bowstring back until it was fully drawn and set. The

209

stake pushed backward into the groove of the crossbow barrel, the whole thing taking a moment or less.

Only one more shot...

I twisted my body around like a snake shedding its skin. The loaded crossbow in my hand pointed straight at Andrew's chest. He was halfway down the stairs. I lay in the hall. We were frozen, two figures in a macabre painting. Andrew broke the spell first.

He began walking down towards me, his hands held out.

'Heather, don't...Please...Trust me...' he began softly.

I pulled the trigger.

Thirty-Eight

He tumbled heavily down the remaining stairs. I could smell blood. I knew I'd never smell anything else again.

Panicking, I scrambled backwards using my forearms. He fell in the exact same spot I'd just left. He didn't move. It had to be a trick. I shuffled right away and struggled to sit up. I stood slowly, expecting him to spring at me again – at any second. Still he didn't move. I could see him. He was lying face down, statue still.

Lights. I *needed* the lights on. If I couldn't have daylight, at least I had electricity. My night vision terrified me. It wasn't real somehow. It wasn't *ordinary*. My sanity needed something ordinary to hold on to. The lights would bring normality and reality back to me.

I stumbled along the walls to the cellar door just before the kitchen, my head spinning. All the bones in my body were turning to warm jelly. It was a struggle to stop myself from passing out. I made it to the main electricity fuse box and reached out to flick the ON/OFF switch.

Yellow-white light cloaked me. I stumbled out of the cellar, shutting the door behind me. Then I leant my head against it briefly.

'Let it be over now.' My plea was whispered.

I turned around – and screamed. Andrew was standing right in front of me. I held my hands out to ward him off, staring terror-stricken at him.

He sank to his knees before falling over sideways on to the ground. Only then did I see the blood staining the left side of his shirt like a huge inkblot.

My aim was true . . .

He reached out with his hand. I didn't move. Then he did a strange thing. He smiled. I backed away.

'Heather, I . . . love you . . .' He coughed. Blood bubbled out of his mouth, trickling down his cheek.

An eternity passed.

'I love you too, Andrew,' I said at last. 'But that's not enough. And it's not good enough. Understand?'

Andrew didn't move, didn't smile, didn't speak. I wondered if he could even hear. I slid down the wall, pulling up my knees in order to rest my head on them. I wrapped my arms around my shins, watching him. Watching him until his eyes glazed over and closed. Then I went over and, sitting with his head in my lap, I cried for both of us.

I looked up towards the ceiling, the roof, the sky, beyond. I felt frozen. Not empty, just numb. As I looked down again, I caught a glimpse of myself in the hall mirror. I could see my reflection. It was only hazy. A misty form, but definitely there. And I couldn't see Andrew's. I hugged his body closer to me. In the mirror he didn't exist. Only me. Some part of me, a deep, almost forgotten part of me, still held a trace of humanity. And I could see it reflected in the mirror.

'So what happens now?' I asked my own reflection.

Maybe I could seek out others like me. But maybe I could do some good, somehow, and work my way back. I'd settle for just pulling myself out of hell.

Above me I heard Morgan groan, then groan again, louder. He was coming round. I looked down at Andrew. I kissed him, slow and sad. Then I let him go.

I stood up and left the house, closing the door behind me.